Sabrina had
stripped nake
but her husband was way ahead.

He was shamelessly making love to her with that slumberous dark gaze of his, heating her blood with a potent mixture of fire and pure masculine chemistry, making her skin prickle with the sensation of being physically touched in the most intimately erotic way. Inside her robe her nipples peaked, the intense aching throb bordering on pain. Moisture spread between the juncture of her thighs as her knees started to shake.

'You should go.' Finding her voice, she silently acknowledged it had no real conviction. How could it when she craved him like parched land needed rain?

'We never kissed when we exchanged vows.' He took a step nearer until her startled gaze was in direct line with the second white button on his shirt. The exposed V of his skin appeared very bronze and all the more appealing because of it. The heat they were engendering between them turned up the temperature in the room another notch.

'I would very much like to remedy that, Sabrina.'

For several years **Maggie Cox** was a reluctant secretary who dreamed of becoming a published author. She can't remember a time when she didn't have her head in a book or wasn't busy filling exercise books with stories. When she was ten years old her favourite English teacher told her, 'If you don't become a writer I'll eat my hat!' But it was only after marrying the love of her life that she finally became convinced she might be able to achieve her dream. Now a self-confessed champion of dreamers everywhere, she urges everyone with a dream to go for it and never give up. Also a busy full-time mum, who tries constantly *not* to be so busy, in what she laughingly calls her spare time she loves to watch good drama or romantic movies, and eat chocolate!

This is Maggie's third book for Modern Romance. Her recent titles are:

THE MARRIAGE RENEWAL
A PASSIONATE PROTECTOR

A CONVENIENT MARRIAGE

BY

MAGGIE COX

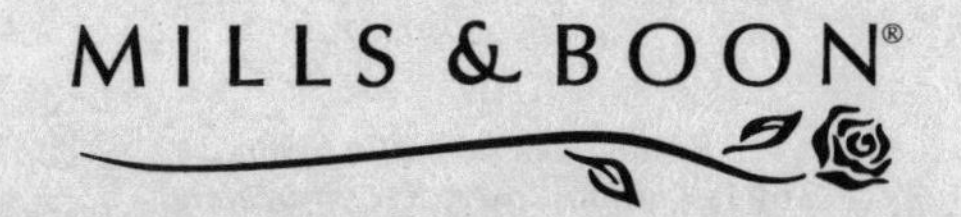

To Ruth and Graham—
I feel so blessed to know you both—and Jean,
who loved to read romance. I miss you still.

First published in Great Britain 2003
Harlequin Mills & Boon Limited,
Eton House, 18-24 Paradise Road, Richmond, Surrey TW9 1SR

ISBN 0 263 83707 6

Set in Times Roman 10½ on 12¼ pt.
01-0104-46712

Printed and bound in Spain
by Litografia Rosés, S.A., Barcelona

CHAPTER ONE

'FAT lot of good *you* did me!' Disparagingly, Sabrina Kendricks glared at herself in the tailored burgundy suit she'd splashed a couple of hundred pounds she couldn't afford on, and knew she'd have to be clean out of every piece of clothing she possessed before she could bring herself to ever wear it again. Dressing to impress had sadly failed to have the desired effect on Richard Weedy—the pompous, halitosis-afflicted excuse for a bank manager whom she had met less than an hour ago. Weedy of stature and weedy by nature as far as Sabrina's assessment was concerned. Spineless, in fact.

'You're not a good risk, Miss Kendricks,' he'd whined. *Not a good risk?* She'd run East-West Travel for fifteen years now, so what was he talking about? What did he want—a cast-iron guarantee? Business was all about taking risks, surely? Good job she didn't have a cat because right now she'd kick it.

Instead, she padded into the kitchen in her stockinged feet and peered hopefully into what she already knew was an empty fridge. Empty because she hadn't had time to shop, and because food seemed to be low down on her list of priorities when she was in dire need of some proper investment to bring her small company in line with twenty-first-century technology. The mere thought of the task that lay ahead haunted her into the early hours. She wasn't going to let the business she'd worked so hard to establish get swallowed up by the big boys who were currently monopolising the travel industry.

Thinking back on her recent interview, she wondered if she'd come across as too hopeful or just simply desperate? She made a face at the bereft shelves, slammed the door shut and went across to the sink to pour herself a glass of water instead. She thought she'd pitched it just right, but maybe her smile had been too forced? Maybe the way she'd pinned back her hair had been too severe? Maybe Moroccan-red lipstick had come across as somehow intimidating? And maybe Richard Weedy just had a thing about pushy career-woman types, as her mother referred to women who didn't permanently wander round the house with a pinny on and a duster in their hands.

Thinking about her mother gave Sabrina indigestion and made her realise that not a morsel of food had passed her lips since six-thirty yesterday evening. It was now just after eleven-thirty in the morning and she was beginning to feel quite nauseous. Maybe it was time to change her bank? Could she do that? One thing was certain, no pinch-faced, patronising, woman-resenting bank manager was going to stop her from making East-West Travel the unalloyed success she knew it could be. She'd sell every pair of shoes she owned and go barefoot before she let that happen.

'Don't go, Uncle Javier! Please don't go!' The slender eleven-year-old with the liquid brown eyes and plaited black hair held on tight to her tall, broad-shouldered uncle, her tenacious grip surprisingly powerful for a child so slight, the plea in her voice and the pain in her expression cutting Javier's heart in two. Above the child's head, his own dark gaze sought out her father, and, looking back at him, Michael Calder's face was nothing less than haunted.

'Hush, Angelina, hush, my angel,' Javier crooned against his niece's hair. 'I was only going to make a phone call to cancel my meeting. I will stay with you as long as you want me to, if that is all right with your father?'

Michael's silent nod was curt but hugely relieved. Both father and daughter were facing a situation that was possibly going to tear the little family apart, and Javier shared doubly in their turmoil because Angelina's mother had been his beloved sister Dorothea, who'd died eight years ago when Angelina was only three. Now the child was facing the possible death of her father. How cruel was that? Just yesterday Michael Calder had been diagnosed with a particularly devastating form of cancer and his prognosis was not good. Tomorrow he would go into hospital for some radical treatment and only God knew how long he would be staying in…maybe he would never come out again. Javier bit back the black thought and concentrated on the weeping child instead. Around her, his embrace tightened. Michael should not have to bear this burden alone. Javier vowed he would do everything in his power to ease their suffering. He would try and bring some stability to Angelina's young life when all around her were shifting sands, as well as being a good friend and support to her father. But first he had to find a way of staying in the UK permanently because as an Argentine national he would need permission to reside.

'I'll get Rosie to make you up a bed.' Unable to bear the sight of his daughter's distress any longer, Michael went in search of their friendly Welsh nanny, clearly thankful for the distraction.

'Let us go and find a video to watch together, hmm?' Holding his niece slightly apart so that he could furnish her with a smile, Javier wiped her tears away then took her gently by the hand into the family's sumptuously furnished living-room.

He woke up to rain. It was pelting his bedroom window with a vengeance, like a hundred small boys firing missiles from catapults. But it wasn't the sight of grey skies and rain that made Javier's heart feel heavy. Angelina had cried herself to sleep. At eleven years of age, she already knew what losing a parent meant. Her uncle had stayed with her long into the night just listening to her breathing, praying with everything he had in him for God to send her peaceful dreams—dreams that weren't possessed with darkly terrifying images of grief and loss. He had left Michael in the living-room nursing a thick glass of single malt whisky—too mentally shattered himself to suggest his brother-in-law should lay off the drink, considering the circumstances. They couldn't go on like this. *Something was going to break if they didn't find a solution soon…*

The smooth tanned lines on his forehead puckering into a scowl, Javier got swiftly out of bed and headed for the bathroom. Once he'd showered and dressed, he would have a cup of Rosie's exquisitely made coffee, then go and rouse Michael with a cup. The man would have one hell of a hangover, that was certain, but then wasn't he entitled? How would *he* feel if he were facing such a bleak future? Scowling again as the family's problems seemed to mount in his head, Javier turned the shower dial to hot then quickly stripped off his clothes.

'OK, so he turned you down, it's not the end of the world.'

Only her sister could come out with such a throw-away remark in the midst of her sibling's disappointment and worry, Sabrina reflected in exasperation as she got down on her knees to play 'peek-a-boo' with the baby. Sometimes she wondered if motherhood had somehow blunted Ellie's perception of how it really was out there in the working world. Once a high-flyer herself, now mother to three lively children under the age of five, Ellie seemed to wrap every problem in a soft-focus cloud of pink, and her adoring husband Phil did nothing to disillusion her.

'Maybe not to you.' Sabrina tickled baby Tallulah under the chin then reached for a baby-wipe to clean the drool off her fingers. 'But it's my livelihood we're talking about here. If I don't get the investment I need then I'm never going to be able to bring the business up-to-date. It will just be a matter of time before we have to fold. And what about Jill and Robbie? They'll be unemployed. Great thanks that would be after all their years of service!'

Ellie stopped her ritual picking up after the two toddlers to shake her head at Sabrina.

'I can't see the fascination myself. It's a dog-eat-dog world out there, Sabrina. Haven't you had enough of the treadmill after fifteen years? You're what now, thirty-seven? Soon you'll be too old to have children, then what? Cold comfort your business is going to be when you have nothing but an empty flat to come home to.'

'You're beginning to sound just like Mum.' Picking up Tallulah, Sabrina nuzzled her affectionately behind her ear, the scent of talcum powder and six-month-old baby giving her heart an unexpected squeeze.

'She only wants you to be happy.'

'I *am* happy, for God's sake! Why is it both of you can't see that I'm doing what I want to do? I'm not like you two; I'm just not the maternal type.'

'No?' Grinning widely, Ellie absorbed the picture of her pretty older sister cuddling baby Tallulah to her supple, willowy frame as if she'd been born to the task.

'Anyway,' Sabrina retorted defiantly, 'I haven't the hips for it.'

'Oh, no? I've seen the looks you get from men when you walk down the street, and believe me—you go in and out in all the right places. What I can't quite believe is that you haven't had a date for at least a year now, maybe more. Are all the men you come into contact with blind, as well as dead from the waist down?'

'I don't have time to date. The business takes up practically every waking hour.'

'Now, that's a sad indictment of a young woman's life.' Wagging her finger, Ellie scooped up a handful of soft toys that littered the carpet and dropped them into the baby's playpen. 'Forget the business for a while. Get yourself a date and go out and have some fun. That's my answer to your present dilemma.'

'Is that the time?' Grimacing at her wrist-watch, Sabrina got hastily to her feet, plonked the baby back into her mother's arms, paused to kiss each of the toddlers sitting in front of the TV, and headed for the front door. 'I'll ring you later. Sorry I've got to dash but I must get back to relieve Jill for lunch. The woman's been in since eight and hasn't had a bite yet.'

'Well, I'm giving you my advice whether you want it or not!' Ellie called after her as she hurried towards the compact gun-metal-grey car parked in the drive. 'Find yourself a date and soon!'

With her sister's undoubtedly well-meant advice ringing in her ears, Sabrina reversed out of the drive into a wide avenue and headed towards town. 'Get myself a date,' she muttered irritably as she fiddled with the radio dial. 'Like I don't have enough problems already without adding a man to the mix!'

Wrestling with her umbrella as well as her now soggy packet of sandwiches and her shoulder bag, Sabrina didn't see the man standing in front of East-West Travel's shopfront peering in until she was almost on top of him. As a strong arm reached out to steady her, she was engulfed in the lingering fragrance of expensive male cologne and a surprising heat that seemed to tinglingly transmit itself right through her body from the brief but firm exchange of contact.

'I'm so sorry. I didn't see you there—I don't normally try to mow people down with my umbrella.' When she'd folded it, transferred her damp packet of sandwiches to her shoulder bag and brushed her brown hair from her eyes, Sabrina gave the man her full attention. Something inside did a funny little flip when she did. *He was gorgeous.* That was the only adjective that came to mind. Tall and Latin-looking with jet-black hair and eyes to match. Eyes that were so dark they glimmered back at her like perfect onyx jewels. When he didn't reply she felt suddenly foolish—foolish and unprepared...but unprepared for what? To cover her embarrassment she gushed, 'If you're looking for somewhere warm at this time of year, Tenerife is always a good bet. I can put you in touch with some wonderful little family-run hotels, or if you wanted something a little more upmarket I could personally recommend some stunning places.'

When he still didn't reply, Sabrina had a couple of bad moments of sheer panic. Perhaps he didn't speak English? Perhaps he was looking at her wondering what this mad woman with the dripping hair and soggy sandwiches was blathering on about?

'Oh, well.' Thinking she'd better make a hasty retreat before she made a complete twit of herself, she shrugged good-naturedly, delivered one of her sunniest smiles and pushed at the shop door to go inside.

'Wait.'

Funny how one softly enunciated little word could convey such innate command. 'I beg your pardon?'

'I would very much like to come inside and discuss a vacation with you.'

'Well, great. Why don't you follow me inside out of this rain?'

Jill had her coat on and her umbrella at the ready behind her desk. The blonde's keen gaze positively lightened when she saw the dazzling specimen of manhood who walked in behind her boss. 'Hi. It's all been very quiet since you've been gone. I sent Rob out to lunch fifteen minutes ago—was that OK?'

'Sure, Jill. You go out and get something yourself now. I'll be fine here.'

'OK. You be good, now.' With a brief conspiratorial wink, the blonde swept past them both and the doorbell jangled behind her.

'Take a seat. I'll just get rid of my coat.' Silently appreciative of the fug of warmth that enveloped her after the cold outside, Sabrina smiled again at the man as she made to dash into the little office at the end of the room. Javier hesitated, his astute business sense automatically kicking in as he scanned the small but neatly presented room with its three old-fashioned desks planted side by side, with an equally old-fashioned computer terminal positioned on top of each one. What was that word the English liked to use when describing something traditional rather than modern? 'Quaint', he thought it was. Yes, quaint. He smiled back at the woman who'd careened into him with her umbrella and registered that her eyes were startlingly blue and guileless…almost untainted by life.

'You must eat your lunch as we talk,' he instructed, and the guileless blue eyes shone back at him in surprise.

Sabrina could hardly believe a stranger was capable of such consideration. A little burst of warmth spread inside her. 'I'll make some coffee,' she replied. 'Would you like some?'

'Black—no sugar. Thank you.' Javier positioned

his tall frame in a padded chair nearest to the office. Silently he watched her through the open door, marking her hurried movements. He saw her remove her coat and hang it on an old wooden coat-tree, saw her hand pat the back of her golden-brown hair encased in its slightly awry knot and registered that she was very pleasingly built beneath the rather plain blue suit and white blouse. Even several feet away from her, her light floral perfume lingered, insinuating its way past his defences and making him feel surprisingly at ease. Astounding when his heart and head were in such turmoil over Angelina and her father. Michael had insisted the child attend school today and at three-thirty Rosie would pick her up and take her to a friend's for tea. 'Best keep everything as normal as possible,' Michael had instructed him. Javier intended to be back at the house to greet her when she came back from her friend's—by which time he would surely have had news of the outcome of his brother-in-law's treatment?

'There you are.' Registering the slight rattle of the cup in the saucer as she placed the coffee carefully down in front of him, Sabrina noted there were no rings on his fingers and his hands were very slender and very brown. And that accent of his—she couldn't quite place it; South American perhaps, but which country?

Sliding behind her desk, she drew her own mug of steaming coffee towards her. Self-consciously unwrapping her sandwiches, she gathered up the cling film into a little ball and jettisoned it into a nearby bin.

'I hope you don't mind?' she checked again before

taking a ladylike bite of her chicken sandwich. 'I didn't actually have any breakfast and to tell you the truth I'm starving!'

'Go ahead. One cannot properly conduct business on an empty stomach.' His lips parted in a brief smile. His teeth were very white against his tan, and movie-star perfect. For the first time she noticed he had a dimple in his chin…a very sexy little dimple. Somehow her morsel of food had trouble getting past her throat.

'So…any ideas where you'd like to go?'

'Excuse me?'

'On holiday? I presume you're thinking of taking a break somewhere?'

Javier shrugged his broad shoulders and wondered what the perfectly English Miss—he squinted at the name on the small gold badge on her lapel—Sabrina Kendricks would think if she knew he had travelled the globe more times than she'd find it easy to believe. As a man who'd built up a successful one-stop travel business on the internet, he spent a large majority of his life travelling. No, he didn't need a holiday. What he needed right now was a little more complicated than that…

'Are you usually this quiet?' Ignoring her question, Javier posed another one. As he did so he glanced curiously around him, noting the colourful posters of varying exotic locations on the walls behind her, the two tall potted plants that resembled miniature palm trees by the door, the once rich maroon carpet beneath his feet that was more than just a little faded. The whole business had an air of regal deterioration about it. Rubbing his hand round the back of his neck,

Javier sighed. Her computer system looked badly out of date, too. How on earth were they making a living?

Sabrina took a hasty sip of coffee, nearly scalding her mouth in the process. 'It's raining,' she explained as if he should understand the unspoken meaning without her elucidating further.

'That puts people off?' His lips quirked wryly. The woman was blushing and it intrigued him as to why.

'It's a slow time of the year.' Shrugging, she glanced quickly away from his too knowing black eyes.

'I should have thought many people would be booking vacations leading up to Christmas. The prospect of getting away after such a hectic time would appeal to most, no?'

He said it as if he knew what he was talking about and Sabrina felt herself grow prickly and defensive. She could hardly tell him that the bigger travel chains that dominated most high streets nowadays naturally took most of the business. But then they couldn't offer the very personal, specialist, highly skilled service that Sabrina and her colleagues had perfected over fifteen years, could they? The chains didn't have time to devote to planning sometimes elaborate itineraries for their wealthier, more established clients—not when they wanted to shift as many cheap package holidays as possible. If Sabrina wanted to compete, it looked as if she would have to go that way too.

'It's not always as quiet as this.'

'I have offended you.' Javier heard the slight quiver in her voice with genuine remorse, saw the wave of pink that shaded her cheeks.

'No.' Putting down her half-eaten sandwich,

Sabrina patted her lips with her paper napkin. For some reason a picture of the loathsome Richard Weedy floated into her mind and she heard him say again that she wasn't a good risk so he wouldn't be recommending the loan. She'd walked out of the bank feeling as if she'd gone to him with a begging bowl. Ugh!

'I'm just not having a very good day. Nothing to do with anyone else but my own sorry inability to rise above my disappointment.'

Inexplicably, Javier's gaze went to her fingers. Her hands were pretty and small but minus a ring of any description. 'Someone hurt your feelings…a man, perhaps?'

It took only a couple of seconds for his comment to click. 'Not in any romantic sense, no.' She was smiling now, her blue eyes shining with humour, and Javier realised that, with her high cheekbones and generous mouth, she was really quite exquisite. *She'd be even more exquisite if she let that hair of hers down…* Now, where had that thought come from?

'Anyway. Back to business. If you don't want a holiday, Mr—er—?'

'D'Alessandro—Javier D'Alessandro.'

He said it so beautifully that Sabrina was instantly transported to another time and place; somewhere very different from chilly, dreary London, somewhere with a landscape of burnt sienna and hot sun, a place where conquistadores ruled the land, conjuring up pictures of glamour and adventure. A place where her current concerns and worries disappeared like magic beneath the hypnotic gaze of a dark-skinned, dark-eyed lover…

'If you don't want a holiday, Mr D'Alessandro, then what can I do for you?' Unconsciously her tongue wetted the seam of her lips. Javier's eyes seemed to grow darker still as he registered the fact.

'I'd like to take you to dinner.' How long had that little thought been going round in his head? Javier wiped his palms down the thighs of his expensive Savile Row suit. He concentrated for a few seconds on her name badge. 'Can I call you in a few days, Sabrina? Right now I have some important business to take care of.'

'Dinner?' For a crazy moment she wondered if she'd heard him right. Good-looking strangers didn't usually just walk in off the street and ask her for a date. Her shoulders stiffened slightly with suspicion.

'Yes, dinner. What do you think?'

'Not a good idea.' Picking up her pen, she scanned the loose papers on her desk for something that needed her attention—anything that would distract her from the quiet scrutiny of those disturbing dark eyes. 'I don't date people I don't know, Mr D'Alessandro.'

'Ahh.' His smile was fleeting yet uncomfortably knowing. 'You're not a risk-taker, then, Sabrina?'

She thought about the business; about the fact that her bank manager thought she wasn't a good risk. Now this handsome stranger in front of her seemed to be implying she was lacking in courage too. It was suddenly all too much. 'All right, Mr D'Alessandro, I will accept your invitation to dinner…whenever that may be. Thank you.' She scribbled something indecipherable on a piece of paper and hoped he didn't notice that her hand was trembling slightly. ‘Get yourself a date!’ Ellie had called out to her only a short while ago. Well, it looked as if she’d got herself one…whether she’d planned for it or not.

CHAPTER TWO

HE DIDN'T call and she shouldn't have been either surprised or disappointed but perversely Sabrina was both. Ever since she'd set eyes on the handsome and intriguing Javier D'Alessandro, she'd been oddly unsettled and discontented. Which wasn't like her at all. Sighing heavily, she gave her make-up one final check in the bathroom mirror, flicked off the light and returned to the living-room to collect her suit jacket and raincoat. The force of the rain outside was rattling the window-panes and a helpless wave of despondency washed over her. Yesterday, she, Robbie and Jill had been practically fighting over customers, they were so few. The day had dragged endlessly on, and when six o'clock came Sabrina had actually been glad to put on her coat and head for home. In fifteen years of running East-West Travel she had rarely been so eager to leave the office. Maybe Ellie was right? Maybe she should call it a day as far as the business was concerned. Concentrate on other things instead. Like finding a potential 'Mr Right' and perhaps having a child of her own before it really was too late. She really loved her sister's kids and she probably wouldn't make the worst job of raising her own. Would she?

'Sabrina Kendricks, where is your head?' Amazed at the winding and not entirely welcome path her thoughts had taken her down, she donned her jacket and coat, retrieved her prized umbrella that she'd bought from an exclusive Knightsbridge store in the sales, then slammed the flat door behind her with enough force to rattle every window in the whole house.

'Call for you, Sabrina! And I've left your coffee on the side; don't let it go cold, will you?'

Waving the receiver at her, Jill waited patiently as Sabrina made her way into the cramped little room that served as general 'all-purpose' filing cabinet and was also a repository for foreign exchange, petty cash and stationery. They also kept a small fridge for milk and juice, and the most essential item of all—the kettle.

'Thanks, Jill.' Not many people called her on what she thought of as her private line. Just a handful of people had the number, namely her parents and Ellie and an old schoolfriend who she kept in touch with from time to time.

Spying her coffee, she lifted the mug to her lips and took a sip before speaking. 'Sabrina Kendricks.'

'Miss Kendricks, this is Javier D'Alessandro.'

She couldn't prevent the breathy little gasp that came out of her mouth. She'd forgotten that she'd given him this number as well as her home one. Carefully, she placed the mug back on the cluttered pine shelf that was crammed with box files, fearful she would spill it because her hand was shaking.

'Mr D'Alessandro...what can I do for you?'

'A short break in Tenerife perhaps? Los Christianos maybe. In one of your charming little hotels that guarantee rest and relaxation and salve to the spirit...'

Oh, my. He could read the Oxford English Dictionary *out loud and it would sound sexy.*

'Really? So you changed your mind about a holiday, then?' Perversely, Sabrina didn't want to talk to him about holidays. She chewed at her fingernail, grimacing at the flaked pearl nail-polish that she'd been too tired to replace last night; another uncharacteristic decision.

'I make a jest with you, Miss Kendricks…Sabrina. I don't want a holiday. I asked you out to dinner, remember?'

'Three weeks ago,' she blurted unthinkingly, then cursed herself for perhaps revealing too much. Now he would think she'd been counting the days.

'I am sorry it has been so long. There were things—family concerns—that I needed to take care of.'

'I understand.' Was he married? Going through a divorce? Did he have kids? A thousand questions backed up in her brain—after all, she knew nothing about this man except that he was too gorgeous for words with black eyes that made her think of things she hadn't considered in a very long time. And young. Don't forget that, Sabrina. He probably wasn't even thirty, and here she was, fast approaching thirty-eight. The whole thing was ridiculous. Best keep her mind on work and not let herself be so foolishly disappointed.

'Would this evening be too short notice?' Javier was suggesting. 'If you give me your address I could pick you up at, say, eight o'clock if that is convenient?'

Sabrina swallowed hard. 'Perhaps it wouldn't be such a good idea for us to meet, Mr D'Alessandro; I—'

'Javier. Please call me Javier.'

'All right…Javier, I don't want you to feel obliged to ask me to dinner just because it seemed like a good idea three weeks ago. I understand how things can change.'

'Then you are a very tolerant woman, Sabrina, but I seriously would like to take you out to dinner and I do not understand this ''feeling obliged'' you talk about. My only motivation is to see you again. I sense that we may have more in common than you think.'

She heard the faint thread of humour in his voice and let out a long, slow breath. 'All right, then. You've talked me into it.' *As if I needed to be persuaded.* Sabrina allowed herself a grin and told him she would prefer to meet him outside the designated restaurant. Once she got the details, he bid her a slightly formal goodbye and told her he was looking forward to their meeting. As Sabrina replaced the receiver on its rest, she went mentally through the contents of her wardrobe and—apart from that disastrous burgundy suit—tried to remember the last time she had bought herself something really nice to wear. The sort of 'something' that would be suitable to wear to a very elegant restaurant in Knightsbridge with a man who would make Hollywood stars look plain.

'I wish you weren't going out tonight, Uncle Javier. I wish you were staying in with me and Rosie.' Angelina glanced up from the television screen as her uncle came into the room, her dark eyes noting how handsome he looked in his suit and tie, his black hair gleaming beneath the soft lamps that lit the room. The slender blonde in her faded jeans and pink sweatshirt, sitting on the luxuriously thick rug beside the child, also marked his entrance with appreciative china-blue eyes.

'Your uncle deserves a night out, Angelina,' she said softly. 'He's stayed in with us every night since your father went into hospital. If you're good you can stay up half an hour longer and watch the end of the film with me.'

'Thanks, Rosie.' Javier flashed her one of his most dazzling smiles and Rosie couldn't help wishing that she was the lady he was taking out tonight. She'd gleaned that his dinner date was a woman named Sabrina because she'd heard him explaining to Angelina. *Lucky Sabrina.*

'I won't be late. I'll look in on the little one here before I go to bed. If you hear anything from the hospital…anything at all, you've got my cellphone number, haven't you? I'll keep it with me.'

'Of course.'

'Now, you be a good girl for Rosie, *mi angel.* Tomorrow after school I will take you to the movies to see that film you have been longing to see. We will eat popcorn and ice cream and forget about everything else but having a good time. *Sí?*'

'Yes, Uncle.' Angelina angled her cheek affectionately for his kiss and at the last minute flung her strong little arms around him and gave him a fierce hug. Javier's heart went 'bump', as it was apt to do every time his beloved niece demonstrated her love for him.

'Sleep well.'

'Tell Sabrina I said hello,' Angelina quipped as he reached the door. Javier smiled.

'I will be sure to tell her,' he promised and left the two females to their television programme, feeling just a little more at ease than he had for the past few nights.

'So you started up the business fifteen years ago?' Javier concentrated his full attention on his dinner companion. How could he not when she was looking animated and beautiful in her scoop-necked scarlet blouse and slim-fitting black trousers, her gorgeous golden-brown hair rippling unhindered to her waist, every bit as lovely as he'd imagined it would be?

'I know, fifteen years…makes me sound as old as Methuselah.'

'But you don't *look* as old as Methuselah,' Javier charmingly assured her. Was she sensitive about her age—this woman with her smile as bright as sunlight and eyes the same stunning blue as a summer sky? She could be no more than thirty-four or thirty-five, surely, and even if she was, what did he care? A woman with a past was always far more interesting, he found, than some inexperienced twenty-year-old who didn't know her own mind.

'I feel it sometimes.' A cloud seemed to slide across the dazzling blue irises. Pouring some more wine into her glass, Javier frowned. 'Something is troubling you. Want to talk about it?'

Sabrina hesitated. Should she burden this charming, good-looking man with her problems at work? The trouble was, he was so easy to talk to. Already she felt as if she'd known him much longer than the two occasions they'd met. After a generous sip of wine to fortify her blood, she decided to go with her instincts. 'I promise not to let my troubles dominate the evening.' She smiled and Javier leant forward, intrigued, his own profound concerns about his family momentarily suspended.

'My problem is that the business needs to expand, come fully into the twenty-first century, and I can't raise the capital to do it. We're even losing some of our oldest customers because they've been lured by the tempting promises of all kinds of incentives by the chains, incentives we can't possibly match. Our equipment is outdated and old-fashioned and the day we met I'd just been turned down by the bank for a loan. At this point I've got two very loyal staff members who've been with me practically since I started and I feel so bad that, unless I can raise some money to modernise soon, they'll both be out of a job.'

'I see.' His eyes were impossibly dark, Sabrina reflected, her heartbeat racing suddenly. It was the wine, she told herself. She'd better take it easy. More than a couple of glasses and she might—just might—make a complete fool of herself…

'If I owned a house I'd put that up as collateral but, as I only rent my flat, that isn't a possibility.' Shrugging, she tried to dismiss her worries and focus on the man in front of her instead. She'd come out to enjoy herself, not bring everything down by talking about work. Ellie was probably right. She was too fixated on her job. She'd almost forgotten how to have fun.

'This wine is delicious. Thank you so much for

asking me out for the evening. I'm really enjoying myself.'

'You are very passionate about your business…and loyal to your staff. I admire that, Sabrina.'

'And what about you, Javier? What are your passions in life?'

'Don't you know you can't ask someone from my country such a question without the same answers?'

'And that is?'

'Argentina. I'm from the capital city—Buenos Aires—and my passions are football, politics and—until very recently—living life in the fast lane.' One corner of his beautiful mouth hitched slightly upwards as if the confession pained him. Even with the wine heating her blood, Sabrina couldn't fail to pick up on the sudden sadness in his voice. Immediately she felt guilty. They'd spent most of the evening so far talking about her. She wasn't usually such selfish company—at least she prayed not.

'So.' She fixed him with such a direct gaze that Javier suddenly experienced a very disorienting feeling of light-headedness. 'Something must have happened to change that? Life in the fast lane, I mean.'

Brought back to earth with a bump, Javier felt his stomach muscles knot painfully as he remembered Michael in hospital, Angelina crying herself to sleep and his own life thrown into the worst kind of personal turmoil yet again in the space of eight short years.

'You are right, something happened,' he said heavily, loosening his tie. 'But it is not something I care to talk about right now.'

'I understand.' Her voice was softly concerned. 'I

just want you to know that if you felt the need to share what was troubling you, I would be a good listener.'

'Of that I have no doubt.' Raising his glass, Javier gave her a small toast. 'I am wondering why you are alone, Sabrina, or am I being too presumptuous? Is there a man in your life?'

'Apart from my horrible bank manager, my colleague Robbie and my lovely brother-in-law, Phil?' Her laugh was uninhibitedly melodic and very, very sexy. The kind of laugh a man didn't easily forget. 'No, Javier. I am footloose and fancy-free…whatever that means. Most of my time is taken up by the business. When I'm there, work just takes over, and when I'm not there I spend most of my free time worrying about it. Boring, aren't I? I don't think many men would put up with that.'

'Men who do not welcome a challenge, perhaps.'

What was he saying? Sabrina thought in fright. Would *he* welcome such a challenge? Her heart did a crazy little dance.

'And what about the future?' he wanted to know, dark eyes speculative. 'Do you see yourself perhaps getting married and having a family?'

It would be too crude to make some flip comment about her biological clock ticking, Sabrina thought, suddenly depressed. Suffice just to tell him no—such a future probably wasn't on the cards for her personally.

'Not really. The business is my baby. Oh, it's not that I don't love kids, I do. It's just that—well, I'm not twenty-something any more and, anyway, I'm probably far too set in my ways for any man to want to take on. How about yourself; do you have a lady in your life? Perhaps at home in Argentina?'

Javier thought about Christina, the 'twenty-something' beautiful Brazilian model he'd been dating up until a couple of months ago—when he'd come home unexpectedly early one afternoon and found her in bed with his twice-married, chain-smoking neighbour, Carlo. He shrugged. 'The lady in my life is eleven years old.' Inevitably a smile found its way to his lips when he spoke about Angelina. He wondered if there was any news from the hospital. He prayed she would get to sleep without tears wetting her pillow tonight.

'You have a daughter?' Blue eyes widening with surprise, Sabrina leant towards him across the table, unknowingly treating him to a very tantalising view of her creamy breasts down the scooped neck of her blouse. Heat raced into Javier's groin and for a moment he was stunned. It had been such a long time since the sight of a beautiful woman could do that to him spontaneously.

He blinked. 'A niece. My sister's child, Angelina.'

'What a pretty name.'

'Yes.'

The waiter interrupted them with their meal. As he bustled about, laying plates on the white rich linen cloth and replenishing their wine, Sabrina sensed there was an air of sorrow about her companion that tugged at her heartstrings and made her want to know what distressed him so. Right now those impressively broad shoulders of his looked weighed down with the worries of the world and she longed to be able to offer even the smallest crumb of comfort.

'Everything looks wonderful.' Picking up her fork, she tried to lighten the mood a little.

Javier smiled that destroyingly slow, thoughtful smile of his that made something in her innermost core clench and tighten with shivery anticipation, and simply said, 'Eat. Enjoy. Then we will talk some more.'

He accompanied her in a taxi home but didn't come in when Sabrina offered him coffee, a nightcap or both. Instead he told her how much he'd enjoyed her company, advised her not to worry about the business because he felt sure something good would turn up, and politely kissed her hand. What threw Sabrina completely was that the charmingly old-fashioned gesture was so unbelievably erotic that her legs were shaking when she finally let herself into her flat and closed the door. Dropping down onto her softly patterned couch with its fading beige and green flowers, she briefly closed her eyes and sighed heavily. He hadn't suggested they see each other again and no doubt she'd blown it by wittering on about the business. A cool, sophisticated, urbane man like Javier D'Alessandro probably thought she was totally boring and one-dimensional, and who could blame him?

When she opened her eyes again she was dismayed to feel tears running down her cheeks. She'd tried so hard to be a success. *So hard.* And all her parents and Ellie were concerned about was when was she going to settle down with a man and have a brood of kids. The fact that she'd successfully run a business for fifteen years meant nothing to them. Suddenly her life seemed all those things she'd accused herself of being and more and she was very, very sorry for it indeed.

Michael rallied after his latest treatment but the doctors told Javier and Michael's mother, Angela, that they mustn't be too hopeful. Too hopeful? The fury Javier experienced in his gut burned him like fire tearing through dry tinder, his Latin temperament rising up in rage against the expected conformity that was supposed to be the acceptable Western reaction to such news. Angela Calder simply squeezed her son's pale, listless hand with her own beringed elegant one and smiled in calm acquiescence. Too ill to notice, even though he'd been much better all day, Michael too seemed to have resigned himself to what he thought of as the inevitable. When Angela briefly quitted the room to go in search of a cup of tea, Michael gestured Javier to his side and told him he had something important to discuss.

'Angelina.' The sick man leant back against the plumped-up white pillows on his hospital bed and forced a smile. Javier immediately felt his throat tighten. It was hard to look at his brother-in-law with all the tubes and medical equipment attached to him without wanting to rip them out and take him home.

'What about Angelina, Michael?'

'I want you to adopt her. You're her closest link to her mother and me. I'd ask Ma but she's not equipped to take care of a child of eleven. She's not strong…a worrier. She let my father do everything until he died. And Angelina doesn't know her that well—she's not exactly been a constant in her life. Not like she knows you, Javier. Will you do that for me, my friend? Will you be a father to my little girl until she grows up?'

There was a burning sensation in his throat and on his lap Javier's knuckles squeezed white. 'It would be an honour, Michael. But you are not going to die…you will get well, *sí*? The hospital, they are doing everything they can to make you well again. Please, do not give up so easily.'

'I'm not giving up. I just know what I know, Javier. Please take care of Angelina and don't take her away from her friends, from all she knows. There must be a way you can stay here. I know it's a lot to ask…your home is in Argentina, but you have a home here too. You've always had a home with us. You know that.' Michael coughed and went deathly pale. Jumping up beside him, Javier gently squeezed his shoulder.

'Michael! Shall I call someone?' He was already turning away, hurrying to the door, pulling it wide and glancing up and down the thickly carpeted corridor for a nurse.

'Javier.'

He returned to Michael's bedside, his heart pounding.

'What is it? I am here.'

'Promise me. Promise me you'll adopt Angelina? I've got to know if you will do this for me.'

Taking the other man's hand in his own, Javier squeezed it as hard as he dared. His chest feeling as if it was in a vice, he managed to dredge up a smile, thinking, *This is too hard, too cruel for anyone to bear; first Dorothea, now Michael.*

'I promise, Michael. I give you my word.'

As the nurse bustled into the room, pushing the drugs trolley ahead of her with a cheery smile that made Javier want to curse, he excused himself, telling his brother-in-law that he needed to get out and get some air—to walk and think and come up with some kind of a plan.

He'd hardly known where his feet were leading him until he found himself outside East-West Travel. There were two other customers in the shop today, one seated opposite the young blonde woman he'd seen on his first visit, and the other engaged in conversation with a man who appeared to be in his late thirties. His brown hair was thinning on top and he wore pale steel-framed glasses that made his colourless face seem even paler. There was no sign of Sabrina. Perhaps she had gone to lunch? Glancing down at his watch, Javier saw that it was just past eleven in the morning. Coffee break, then? He'd never know until he went in and asked.

Jill glanced up in surprise as she recognised the incredibly good-looking male who walked through the door.

'Hello there,' she said cheerily. 'Looking for Sabrina?'

'*Sí.* I mean yes. Is she around?'

'She's in the back.' She pointed vaguely in the direction of the little room at the end. 'Busy doing paperwork.'

'Then I won't disturb her.' Frustrated, Javier went to walk away.

Jill waved him to a stop. 'Don't be silly! There's nothing Sabrina likes better than to be distracted from her paperwork. Go on through. She might even have the kettle on.'

His first glimpse of Sabrina was her back. She was wearing a formal blue skirt and jacket, her delightful hair caught up in some intricate tortoiseshell comb, her stockinged feet bare. At the moment one small, slender foot was easing its way up and down the back of her calf as if to soothe the strain that was there. He heard her proffer up a very unladylike curse beneath her breath as she studied some papers on top of an antiquated steel filing cabinet, and couldn't help but smile.

'Hello there. Your colleague said it was all right if I came through.'

Her heart knocking wildly against her ribs, Sabrina spun round, took one look at Javier D'Alessandro and found her greeting jammed in her throat. Wearing a stylish black coat over black jeans and a navy-blue cashmere sweater, the man looked like a million dollars. The citrus, woody tang of his aftershave wafted round the room, tightening her insides, instinctively making her want to retreat behind her professional mask for protection.

'It's nice to see you again.' Smoothing down her skirt, she smiled. *She was the first good thing that had happened to him all day,* Javier acknowledged. Perhaps it would make it easier to broach the subject he had come to talk to her about? He hoped so.

'You too. I was wondering if we could talk a little?'

Taken aback, Sabrina tucked a stray glossy strand of hair behind her ear. 'Of course. Is here all right? I know it's a bit cramped but I don't really have anywhere else to—'

'I noticed a park across the road.' Javier jerked his head vaguely in that direction. 'Can we take a walk?'

'Why not? I could do with some fresh air, to tell you the truth. I'll just get my coat.'

The winding concrete path into the ornamental gardens was littered with the colourful debris of autumn leaves. As they walked along side by side, Sabrina shivered inside her warm camel-coloured coat, wishing she'd thought to add her scarf to the hastily donned outer clothing. A tremendous gust of wind whooshed past her ear just then, and she shoved her hands deep into her coat pockets and turned her head to grin at the man beside her.

'Tenerife is sounding more and more attractive by the minute, wouldn't you say?' she announced cheerfully. 'Coming from a warm climate, this weather must seem positively Arctic to you!'

'My country has an amazing diversity of climates and landscapes. Don't forget we've got the snow-capped Andes as well as acres of hot, humid jungle. But yes, I do agree, by my home city's standards, it is pretty cold.' As he smiled back at her with something like pleasure in those deep, dark eyes with their straight black lashes, it was still clear that Javier had something on his mind other than the weather.

In for a penny… Sabrina decided to bite the bullet. Best clear the air and get whatever it was he had to say out of the way, then maybe, just maybe, she could suggest they meet for lunch later on in the week? She could practically hear Ellie cheering on the sidelines. Sabrina had *never*—not even once—asked a man out on a date. Well, there was a first time for everything, so they said…

'You wanted to talk. Was it something in particular?'

Spying a weatherworn bench near a thick clump of hedgerow, Javier jerked his head towards it. 'Perhaps it would be better if we sat down?'

For some reason, Sabrina's heartbeat thundered in her chest as she sat down beside him. Where previously they'd been companionable, something in the air had shifted perceptibly and there was a new tension emanating from the big, handsome man sitting next to her. Once again Sabrina shivered, but this time not with the cold.

'I can help you with your business,' he said without preamble.

'What did you say?' She'd heard but couldn't begin to make sense of such a statement.

'I will give you the money—whatever the amount—as well as my expertise and knowledge to help you modernise the business and bring it into the twenty-first century.'

Sabrina's pale hand curled tightly round the wrought-iron arm rest of the bench. 'What's all this about, Javier? I don't understand.'

CHAPTER THREE

HIS expression couldn't have been more serious. Dropping his head briefly into his hands, he drew them back and forth through his thick, dark hair. 'I am also involved professionally in travel. I have a very successful internet business that I have been running for the past six years. I believe I know exactly what it is you need to do to turn East-West Travel around. If you will let me I would like to help you.'

'I'm sorry but you'll have to give me a couple of minutes here.' Completely bewildered, Sabrina considered Javier with stunned blue eyes as if he had suddenly grown fangs and an extra head. 'Am I hearing you right? You are in the travel business and you would be willing to lend me money and your expertise to expand my company? Why? Out of the goodness of your heart? Forgive me if I sound cynical, Mr D'Alessandro, but I'm not as green as I'm cabbage-looking!'

Frowning, Javier tried to make sense of her words. 'I'm afraid you have lost me.'

'You are no more lost than I am, that's for sure!' Her heart beating wildly inside her chest, she folded her arms tightly across her coat and glared at him. 'Is that why you were looking in the window that day? Did you already know about my circumstances? Were you hoping to buy me out for a song, because if you are I can tell you right now, you're on an awfully sticky wicket!'

Javier groaned. His head hurt trying to keep up with her colourful outpouring of injured pride.

'I do not want to buy you out, Sabrina. That is the first thing. It was pure chance that had me standing outside your window that day. I had a lot on my mind and needed to walk and think. I'm staying at my brother-in-law's house, which is not so very far away from you. I suppose I naturally gravitate towards anything to do with travel—like you, I am passionate about it. *That's* why I happened to glance in your window when you ran into me.' He paused to gaze into her pale, anxious face, hoping that his words had reassured her that he wasn't some opportunistic shark waiting to snatch her beloved business out of her grasp.

Her heartbeat returning to a more normal cadence, Sabrina released an audible sigh. 'OK. Go on. I take it there's more?'

He nodded briefly, his long brown fingers linking together on his lap. 'If you agree to let me help you, there is something I would ask of you in return. Something that is not altogether an easy thing for me to ask.'

He didn't have to tell her that. Sabrina guessed whatever it was was causing him great concern and difficulty. As for his incredible offer—the answer to her prayers, no less—well, she wasn't about to jump up and down with joy just yet. She had a natural tendency to be naïve about a lot of things but not this—not her precious livelihood.

'Ask away. I'm listening.' Two pigeons landed a

few feet away, picking hopefully around in the leaves for a bite to eat. When they found nothing they simultaneously flew off into the trees in a brief flurry of wings and foliage. Sabrina pulled up the lapels of her coat around her ears and prayed she wasn't going to be crushingly disappointed by whatever Javier had to say. Already she was beginning to like this man too much for her peace of mind and she couldn't pretend she wouldn't be sorry if she never saw him again.

'I told you I have a niece? Angelina.' Sabrina heard the love in his voice and something warm stirred in the pit of her stomach, something that her heart suddenly ached for. 'She means everything to me. Especially since her mother—my sister, Dorothea—died eight years ago. Now her father, Michael, is ill. Dangerously ill. His prognosis, they tell me, is not good. I would do anything to help Angelina, to keep this terrible hurt from her, a hurt she has already experienced once before in her young life.

'Michael would like me to adopt her. There lies my problem. I do not have permanent residency in this country and, although I can more or less come and go as I please, the courts will not be favourable to my application if I cannot offer Angelina a permanent home here. She is too anglicised to want to live in Argentina, though of course she has grandparents there, family. Plus she would not wish to be separated from her friends. To get straight to the point, Sabrina, I need a British passport to stay here and adopt her. The only way I see I can get that quickly is to marry someone from this country.'

Frowning as the meaning of his words began to

sink in, Sabrina let out a long, slow breath and tucked some windswept strands of honey-brown hair behind her ear. 'You're asking me to—to marry you?'

He unlinked his hands to push his fingers through his hair. 'It would be—what do you call it?—a marriage of convenience. Only on paper, no more. Of course, we would have to live together for a reasonable amount of time to please the courts, but after that…' He shrugged as if it was the most reasonable proposition in the world. 'After that I would, of course, not contest a divorce. You would be a free woman once again.'

'And if I agree to this—this "marriage of convenience"—you agree to help me with the business?' Her whole body felt suddenly terribly cold. A wave of vulnerability settled on her shoulders like a heavy coat. The first man she'd met in the longest time that she'd felt even remotely attracted to and all he wanted from her was a cold-hearted business proposition. Well, that just about summed her personal attributes up nicely, didn't it?

'*Sí.* Yes. You have my word.' Of course. He had to be a man of honour—young as he was. Even on such brief acquaintance, that was never in doubt in Sabrina's mind.

Feeling ridiculously like crying, she got slowly to her feet, turned to Javier and smiled in spite of the fact that her face felt like a block of ice with no movement in it at all.

'I'm sorry, Javier. I couldn't do it.'

'What is it you want in return? How can I persuade you to change your mind? I will double any figure you care to come up with. I am a very wealthy man,

Sabrina. You can check me and my company out on the internet. You say you rent your flat? I will buy you a house of your own for you to keep after we are divorced.'

He was only making it worse. Her heart ached at the thought of that possibly soon-to-be-orphaned little girl—Angelina—but Sabrina couldn't agree to such a bizarre proposition for her sake only…could she? Even if what he had offered her in exchange seemed like the solution to all her worries.

Recognising the anxiety on her face, Javier told himself to ease back—not to push. She would need time. He could see that. She was not the sort of woman who would grab at such an opportunity with no thought of what it might mean to her personally other than the help she needed to expand her business. No. Sabrina Kendricks clearly had a lot of good qualities. Qualities like warmth, tenderness and integrity… He cut himself off short. He wasn't looking for a lifetime partner so such qualities hardly mattered. Nor was he in the market for the kind of marriage that his parents and grandparents and—up until eight years ago—his sister and Michael had enjoyed. What was the point in setting yourself up for potential disaster and misery? He'd seen what love could do. Love could rip away your soul just as soon as your back was turned. That wasn't for him. Instead he would pour all the love he had in his heart into caring for Angelina. If he could do that, then his life wouldn't be wasted.

'I'm really sorry about your niece. It must be terrible to be faced with losing both parents—at any age, never mind eleven years old. But I couldn't do it,

Javier. Please understand. I'm just—I'm just not like that.'

'But you are an astute businesswoman, no?' Pushing himself off the seat, he towered over her. 'How could you throw away the perfect opportunity to save your business? You already told me the bank manager turned you down for a loan. Where else are you going to get the money from, Sabrina?'

'That's my problem.' Flinching from the cold whipping round her ankles, she seriously wondered if it *was* the perfect opportunity. Surely she owed it not just to herself but to Jill and Robbie to do all she could to save their jobs? If Javier D'Alessandro could look on the whole thing as purely a business merger, why couldn't she?

Sensing the conflict that was raging behind those bright blue eyes, he shook his head and decided to go for broke.

'It wouldn't have to be a problem at all if we agreed to make a deal. I'm not asking you to engage your emotions here, Sabrina. It is an emotive issue, I know that, but I am speaking to you as one business-man to another—we have both something to gain; it makes sense, *sí*?'

'I'll think about it.'

Without another word she turned on her heel and hastened back down the path, through the sea of dead leaves, back the way they had come.

Javier stayed where he was for a long time after she had left. He returned to the park bench and stayed there with his head in his hands, his mind working overtime and his gut churning until finally the raw bite of the increasingly cold wind made it impossible for him to stay there any longer. *She would think about it.* It didn't mean she would agree. His heart heavy, he headed back to the house, preparing himself to hear the worst and cursing every fate known to man for the predicament he found himself in.

'I've been ringing you for two days now with no answer. Jill told me you were home with a cold. Why haven't you been answering your phone?' With baby Tallulah on her hip, her light blue eyes unusually fierce, Ellie McDonald barged her way past Sabrina, only noticing that her sister was still in her dressing gown when she plopped herself down on the couch and settled Tallulah against a pile of velvet cushions with her rattle. Not only was Sabrina in her dressing gown but also the room was almost unbearably hot, with the radiators obviously turned up to maximum heat.

Slowly Sabrina came towards her. Pressing her handkerchief to her reddened nose, she smiled uncharacteristically feebly. 'I *have* got a cold,' she said defensively. 'I've been in bed. That's why I didn't answer the phone.'

'But you never get colds!' Ellie sounded cross. 'You're usually disgustingly healthy. What's up, Sabrina? Something must be wrong.'

'Nothing's wrong, other than I've got the mother of all colds.' Crossing to an armchair littered with books and a half-eaten plate of toast, Sabrina weakly cleared away the mess and flopped down, her blue eyes watery. She'd been suffering for a week now, ever since she'd left Javier in the park, contemplating the fate of his beloved Angelina. Racked with guilt and remorse, she'd had three badly sleepless nights before waking up one morning with a head that seemed as though every bell in Canterbury Cathedral was clanging through it, and a mouth so dry it felt as if it were stuffed with straw. Every muscle ached when she moved, and throbbed when she didn't move, and it was all she could do to struggle out of bed and get herself something to drink. She was sick and miserable and, if it was true that there was light at the end of the tunnel, right now she couldn't see anything but a very big black hole.

'Sounds more like flu to me.' Ellie's voice softened. 'Got any paracetamol?'

'In the cupboard in the kitchen.'

'When was the last time you took some?'

'About seven.'

'This morning?' Ellie tucked a couple more cushions around the smiling Tallulah and jumped up, glancing at the clock on the wall as she did so. 'Did you know it's nearly five o'clock? If you're going to get better you need to look after yourself properly.'

'Stop behaving like my mother.'

'Well, here's news for you, darling. In her absence I *am* your mother. She'd kill me if she knew you were in such a state and I did nothing. Don't worry, I don't have to rush back. I've left Henry and William with her and promised I wouldn't come away until I was sure you were all right.'

A hot drink cupped in her hands and the cold medicine duly taken, Sabrina leant back in the armchair and smiled at the gurgling baby nursing in her mother's arms.

'Thanks, Ellie. I'm not usually so disorganised. It's just that this thing has knocked me for six.'

'I can see that! In a minute I'm going to heat you up some chicken soup. Thank God you had some tins in the cupboard—but not much else, as far as I can see. I'll have to do you a shop before I leave.'

'You don't have to—'

'I *do* have to! Stop pretending you don't need any help, sis; it's not a sign of weakness, you know. Sometimes we all need a bit of help.'

Javier needs help…my help, Sabrina thought bleakly. What could it hurt to agree to his proposition? There was no one on her side to object, after all. No adoring boyfriend waiting in the wings to protest. Her family—Ellie and her parents—might have something to say about it, but at the end of the day it was her decision. She was thirty-seven years old and answerable to no one but herself. Just as soon as she was better she would get in touch and tell him. But how? She had no telephone number for him. But there was always the internet. Maybe if she got in touch with someone at his company, they might have a mobile-phone number for him? She could only pray they had because unless he contacted her there was no other way forward. Her mind made up, she made a cooing noise at the baby, then paused to sneeze several times in quick and noisy succession so that Ellie sighed and told her to go back to bed; she would see to everything while she slept. Too weak to disagree, Sabrina did as she was told.

It had rained at the funeral and not for the first time that day Javier heard someone make a pithy comment about it 'only raining on the just.' Whatever that meant. If it meant that Michael Calder had been a good man then they were right. He'd been a doting father and a skilful surgeon and his sister had adored him from the moment she'd set eyes on him. Initially reluctant to let their beloved only daughter settle in a foreign country far away, Javier's parents had eventually come round to the fact that Dorothea was head over heels in love with her new husband so what could they do? There was still a strong thread of chauvinism in the culture, and they believed emphatically that, when all was said and done, a woman's place was with her husband.

A week after the funeral, Javier was never far from Angelina's side, Michael's mother Angela and the distraught Rosie doing their level best to run the house around them. At night, when Angelina at last fell into an exhausted but troubled sleep, Javier continued to monitor his business from the UK, using Michael's office and computer. Although exhausted by grief and worry himself, he welcomed the distraction of work to help him get past the ever-present problem of gaining a British passport and starting adoption proceedings. In spite of the fact that she was obviously unwilling, Javier found he couldn't regret the proposition he'd made to Sabrina. Maybe one day she would understand what had driven him to make such a desperate request. Perhaps he should send her some flowers with a brief note of apology? He truly hoped he hadn't offended her. She was a nice woman. A *good* woman. The kind of woman he was sure could help Angelina smile again, given time. Sighing, he switched off the computer and sat drumming his fingers on the desk. Staring down at the cup of coffee that Rosie had made him an hour ago and was now congealed and cold, he picked up the phone without further thought and dug around in his wallet for her telephone number at home.

On the third ring, Sabrina forced herself out of bed on leaden legs, clicked on the light in the darkened living-room and pushed her dishevelled hair out of her eyes. Glancing at the clock on the wall, she blinked in disbelief at the time. Ten to midnight. What the—?

'Hello?'

'Sabrina.'

'Javier?' She blinked again as her heart started to race.

'I know it is late.'

'What's wrong? What's happened?' She knew it had to be his brother-in-law. Something heavy settled in her stomach.

'I owe you an apology.'

'No, you don't.' She was surprised at the strength in her own voice, taking it as a sure sign that she was well on her way to recovery despite the woolly feeling in her limbs.

'I would have been in touch sooner but Michael died over a week ago and things have not—well, I'm sure you can imagine they are not good.'

'I'm so sorry. I really am. How is Angelina?'

'Devastated. Lost. Frightened. I keep telling myself that there must be a reason for everything that has happened but it is hard to see what it could be. Anyway, I am forgetting my manners. How are you?'

The man could ask after her welfare when he was going through personal hell? Her fingers went white where they were clutching the receiver. 'I'm fine. Just getting over a cold as a matter of fact, but Javier, I—'

'You are keeping warm and eating well?'

She frowned. 'Honestly, I'm fine. I just want to—'

'I would like to see you again before I go back to Buenos Aires. Perhaps I can take you to lunch?'

'You're going back?' Sabrina caught her breath, glanced round helplessly for a tissue to press against her itching nose and wished her mouth didn't feel as if something had died inside it.

'I have to,' he replied heavily. 'I cannot stay indefinitely. Angela—Michael's mother—is going to look after Angelina until I return again, which I hope will be soon. It will have to be this way until I can think of some better arrangement.'

In her mind, Sabrina saw those riveting dark eyes of his deep with pain and she foolishly wished she were with him so that she could offer him solace. Perhaps put her arms around him and ease some of his hurt in the way that only a woman could. Who was she kidding? He didn't want that kind of comfort from her. The only kind of comfort he needed was her agreement to marry him so that he could settle in the UK and get a British passport. At least she could offer him that. Her breath tight in her lungs, she swallowed hard before speaking.

'No, Javier. You don't have to go back. Not if I agree to marry you.'

The sharp intake of breath at the other end was audible. 'What exactly are you saying, Sabrina?'

'I'm saying I agree to your proposition. The one

you made the other day in the park. I'll be your wife, Javier, if that will help.'

'You do not know what this means to me, Sabrina. From the bottom of my heart I thank you.'

'You're welcome.' With a sad little smile flitting across her face, Sabrina knew with certainty that she was doing the right thing. The *decent* thing. As her parents had always drummed into her from an early age. If nothing else, she could surely take comfort in that?

'You do realise I'm almost thirty-eight years old, Javier?' she blurted out suddenly, for God only knew what reason. Maybe to put him off?

To her consternation he chuckled, the warm sound rippling over the telephone lines like a physical caress and sending her temperature even higher than it already was.

'And I am thirty; so what of it? Age is—how do you say?—nothing but a number. It makes no consequence.'

Of course not. Why should it? It wasn't as if they were contemplating a whole future together, was it?

As she gripped the receiver even tighter, Sabrina's voice dropped to a barely audible whisper. 'I just thought you ought to know,' she told him.

The little bunch of freesias looked slightly wilted where she clutched them in her lap in the back of the taxi but their soft, elusive scent was intoxicating and somehow added to the sense of unreality about what she'd done. As Sabrina glanced out of the window past reams of shoppers and office workers on their lunch breaks, she reflected that normally she'd be one of them if she hadn't taken the day off to get married.

Married. She studied the slim gold band encircling her second finger, left hand, and sighed. It seemed so final. Somehow incontrovertible. Which was ridiculous when it wasn't really a marriage at all. Not really. Just a paper contract so that Javier could stay in the UK with his beloved Angelina. What her parents and Ellie were going to say about it all when they found out, she hardly dared imagine. Whatever it was, 'congratulations' probably wasn't going to feature.

'You are cold?' Sensing her shiver, Javier turned to his new wife with a concerned gaze, searching her vivid blue eyes for confirmation. He owed this woman so much—he didn't intend to let her down in any way. He started to remove his coat to give it to her but Sabrina shook her head quickly and smiled.

'I'm fine, really.'

In spite of the unusual circumstances of their marriage Javier had felt a spurt of pride pulse through him as he'd stood by her side in the register office listening to her strong, clear voice repeat her vows. In her cream suit and white silk camisole, her make-up understated but becoming and her honey-brown hair lifted off her nape into a stylish chignon, she looked pretty and sophisticated. His heart beat a little faster when he thought about introducing her to Angelina, knowing he would have to play it very carefully so as not to cause his niece even a moment's anxiety that this unknown English woman might replace her in her uncle's affections. Distracted by thoughts of the child, he silently acknowledged that he was getting used to walking very warily around her. Every day since the funeral had been like a time bomb ticking away, potential disaster looming at every corner. Both her doctor and the children's grief counsellor had told him to give her time, plenty of time to express her emotions or simply keep them to herself. He shouldn't expect too much. It was early days yet and the loss of her father had hit her hard.

With everything he had in him, Javier prayed that one day he might bring a smile to her face again. Maybe Sabrina could help? Glancing back at his new wife, he allowed himself a brief moment of ease. He didn't know her well—how could he on such short acquaintance? But already he had the feeling that those slender shoulders of hers would prove a more than worthy ally if the situation called for it. In return, he would make certain that she got everything she wanted.

'Is this the house?' Sabrina was craning to see out of the window as the taxi pulled up in front of an impressive Edwardian terrace in a very exclusive part of Kensington. Her teeth worried her slightly fuller lower lip as she absorbed what it meant. This was to be her new home for the time being—until Javier found them another, more neutral residence, where he, Angelina and Sabrina might make a fresh start away from the ghosts of yesterday and the tragedy of all that had happened. *At least until he and Sabrina got divorced.* Her stomach lurched a little at the thought. Already she was becoming dangerously attached to the idea of becoming more than just a 'temporary' wife—a thought she'd better quickly divest herself of if she knew what was good for her.

'Come and meet Angelina,' Javier instructed quietly, sliding his hand over hers.

Electricity shooting through her at his touch, Sabrina managed a husky 'OK' before preceding him nervously out onto the pavement.

CHAPTER FOUR

ANGELA CALDER had offered her a cup of tea and been cautiously welcome. Now Sabrina sat with Javier in the bright modern kitchen—some original features from such a dignified old house not withstanding—and sipped at the brew in the delicate porcelain cup feeling as if her equilibrium might be as easily shattered any moment now. The tension between them all was tangible, enforced politeness making Sabrina emit a silent scream of protest somewhere inside her head. She knew they'd suffered the worst tragedy but shouting and crying was surely better than this frozen veneer of coping?

Beside her, Javier had loosened his blue silk tie, removed his coat and jacket and commandeered the sturdy ladder-back chair with his tall, hard-muscled frame as if silently taking stock of all that had happened. Just what was going on behind those brooding, faintly weary dark eyes of his? Once again Sabrina had an almost uncontrollable urge to reach out and offer him comfort—but here, in front of his niece's grandmother? It was easy to sense such a display would go down like a lead balloon. *They* were family and she the interloper, in Angela Calder's eyes an unknown quantity—a loose cannon that could potentially blow them all apart.

'This is a wonderful cup of tea,' she said out loud,

breaking the silence that had fallen round the table. 'Just what I needed.'

'Thank you, dear.' Angela's eyes flicked across to Javier. 'When you're both finished, perhaps you might like to show Sabrina her room, Javier? She might like to put her feet up for five minutes.'

'I'd like her to meet Angelina first. I let her take the day off school so that she would be here when we came back. Why didn't you tell me that Rosie was taking her out to the park?'

It was the first time she'd heard his disapproval and Sabrina studied the handsome, almost sculpted profile of her husband and felt a small shiver run down her spine.

'The child hadn't said two words all morning, just sat in front of the TV watching one of those daft pop-music programmes. Both Rosie and I thought that some fresh air might do her good.'

'No doubt you are right.' Dragging his fingers through his sleek black hair, Javier pushed away from the table and stood up to his full height. He looked deliberately at Sabrina. 'Let me show you your room. Angela is right; you must be tired. You have only just got over a cold.'

I'm not an invalid! Sabrina wanted to reply but bit back her unexpectedly angry retort out of deference to the situation. If anyone was showing the strain of the morning it was Javier—not her. Those broad shoulders of his were presently carrying the weight of the whole planet if his expression was anything to go by.

In the large, bright, decidedly feminine bedroom with its huge canopied bed, flowing voile curtains and walnut furniture, Sabrina perched on the edge of an antique Edwardian chair and glanced up at the man currently pacing the floor. Restless energy was pouring off him in waves, like a trapped tiger prowling its cage.

'Javier?' she ventured quietly. 'Are you having second thoughts about all this?'

Immediately he stopped pacing. A muscle flinched in the side of his smooth, recently shaven cheek.

'No. Are you? This is a big thing for you to have done, Sabrina. I understand you must have many doubts but I will try and ease them one at a time. Will you ring your parents today and tell them what has happened?' In truth, it worried him that she had ventured into this arrangement without apparently telling a soul. He knew it was in reality a temporary arrangement, a marriage of convenience, but it still bothered him that she wouldn't share the news of their union with the people closest to her. What would they think when they found out? Would they believe he had some kind of hold over her? Would they distrust his promise of help with her business? He sighed and rubbed a hand round the back of his neck.

'Of course I'll tell them…my sister too. I can hardly keep it a secret when I won't be at the flat any more. I know this is how it has to be to satisfy the courts that our marriage is bona fide but is this arrangement going to work, Javier? I mean, living here in Michael's house—his daughter's home? What did you tell Angelina about me?'

'I told you. I said that you were a very nice woman who had agreed to a marriage with me so that I could get a British passport and stay in this country. I explained that you would be living with us for a while so that the courts would believe our marriage was real; that it was important for us to be able to convince them.'

Sabrina dropped her gaze to the floor, to the rich powder-blue carpet that she knew her feet would disappear into if she kicked off her shoes. Everything about the house spoke of luxury and wealth. Michael Calder had been a highly skilled surgeon with a practice in Harley Street. It followed that the family had money. She knew that her husband was wealthy too because she had done as he had suggested and found his company on the internet. There had been newspaper and magazine articles posted on the site—'Javier D'Alessandro, young internet entrepreneur—multimillionaire by the age of twenty-eight.' What had he thought of her small, cramped little flat when he'd come to collect her suitcases, with its faded wallpaper and mish-mash of colourful rugs that covered up a carpet that was threadbare and old? She would have liked to perhaps decorate more but because of her devotion to work, barely ever had the time. Oh, well, too late now for recriminations. As she glanced up, her anxious blue eyes careened helplessly into his. 'At least you told her the truth. She won't expect me to…to—'

'Act like a real wife?' A flash of pain stole into his suddenly hard gaze. 'Let me reassure you on that score, Sabrina. I have no intention of holding you to anything other than a purely business arrangement. I have neither the aim nor the desire to infringe that in any way whatsoever, so you can relax. Now I have to go and make some phone calls. Rest or unpack, I don't mind which. I'll bring up your suitcases then leave you in peace until Angelina returns.'

He walked out of the room with a purposeful, almost angry stride, leaving Sabrina bewildered and hurt at the unexpected coldness in his voice.

'Hello there. I'm Sabrina. You must be Angelina.'

The child was drinking a glass of milk, a plate with a sandwich on it next to her elbow. She glanced up at Sabrina's voice, marking her entrance with huge, doe-like brown eyes, watching her for one or two anxiously assessing moments before concentrating once again on her drink.

Wiping her hands down the front of her trousers, Sabrina cautiously approached the table. She hadn't wanted to stay confined to her bedroom any longer and, when Javier hadn't come back for her, decided to show her face without him. At the sink a petite blonde in jeans and blue sweatshirt was rinsing some fruit beneath the tap. 'Hi. I'm Rosie; pleased to meet you. Sit down—I'll get you a cup of tea in a minute, or would you prefer coffee?'

'Coffee would be nice…thanks.'

She pulled out a chair two spaces down from Angelina. 'Did you enjoy your walk in the park?'

'It was OK.' The girl didn't look up from her sandwich. Sabrina's stomach lurched. Oh, God, this was going to be so much harder than she'd even imagined. All she really wanted to do was gather the child into her arms and hold her close. Just as she did with her nephews Henry and William and baby Tallulah when they were scared or hurt.

'Near where I work there's a wonderful park where

I sometimes go to eat my lunch. It has a bandstand and squirrels and a small playground with swings. At this time of the year you can barely see the grass for all the leaves covering it. When I was little I used to love to run through the leaves in the park. I thought it was the greatest fun. Do you ever do that?'

Angelina seemed to consider the question. 'You're not like my uncle's last girlfriend—Christina. She was much skinnier than you.'

And what exactly was she meant to glean from that? Did the child resent Sabrina for marrying her uncle when she would maybe have preferred the skinnier Christina?

'I won't ever be skinny,' she admitted with a smile. 'I like my food too much.'

'But you have a nice figure. Like my dance teacher, Holly. She teaches me ballet and tap.'

The unexpected compliment completely threw Sabrina. 'Really? I'd like to be able to dance but my dad always said I was about as graceful as an elephant!' She grinned at the memory and tried to ignore the little stab of hurt that always accompanied the thought. It was Ellie who had been the graceful one. The one who all the boys had whistled at on the way home from school.

Angelina nodded. 'My daddy loved to watch me dance.' At the drainer, Rosie paused in arranging the newly washed fruit into a thick glass bowl. Sabrina's heart beat a little faster.

'I'm sure he did. He must have been very proud of you. Very proud.'

'You married my uncle today.'

'Yes.' Her face flooded with heat. 'Do you mind?'

Considering the question for what seemed like a lifetime, Angelina eventually shook her head. 'No.'

'No what?'

Newly showered, his black hair glistening sleekly, Javier strolled into the kitchen, his gaze immediately alighting on his niece.

'I said no, I didn't mind you and Sabrina getting married. Can I be excused now, Uncle? I want to go and listen to some music.'

'Sure. Do you like pop music, Sabrina?' He asked the question as if he was genuinely interested in her answer. Perhaps he thought she was too old to enjoy that sort of thing? Willing herself to stop being so damn sensitive about her age around him, she summoned up a grin instead. 'Yeah, I like pop music. I confess I have a real soft spot for some of the boy bands.'

'Me too!' Angelina's eyes lit up at the news and, catching his expression above her head, Sabrina felt Javier's gaze melt thankfully into hers. It gave her heart a real jolt—as if she'd been plugged into a new, mysterious source of power.

'How many CDs have you got, Angelina? I've got a small collection of my own I could let you look through if you'd like?'

'Sure.' She glanced up at her uncle as if to search for his approval. 'If that's all right?'

'If Sabrina says it is, then it is.' Javier walked across the tiled floor to a worktop. He examined the kettle for water then plugged it in. 'Maybe you'd like to show Sabrina your room later. I think she'd be impressed by your own music collection, don't you?'

'OK.' The girl took a bite of sandwich, seemingly satisfied by her uncle's response.

Had she unknowingly jumped a hurdle where Angelina was concerned or was it far too early to tell? Arms folded on the table top, Sabrina sought out Javier as though drawn by some invisible connective cord. What was it about the man that made a room light up when he entered it? No wonder his niece adored him. Had the skinny Christina adored him too? It was none of her business, she decided unhappily. Not when her own presence in his life was destined to be merely the most temporary of arrangements.

'Run that by me again.' Jill was regarding Sabrina as if she'd just told her she'd won the jackpot on the lottery. 'I thought you said you'd got married. Was I hearing things?'

Clicking some papers into place in a large ring-binder, Sabrina paused, flustered, and instinctively knew that her colleague's reaction to her announcement was going to be a mere bagatelle compared to her parents and Ellie. Yesterday she'd been so on edge anyway, what with the ceremony, settling into the house and meeting Angelina, that she had deliberately avoided ringing them, and now the prospect of their disapproval loomed like a collection of stormy grey clouds on the horizon.

'No, you weren't hearing things. I got married. Please don't make it into a big deal, Jill. It's not a love match or anything like that.'

Jill's eyes grew even wider. 'It's not?'

'I've done it to help someone out.' So why was she having palpitations at the mere thought of the man?

'Someone?'

'Javier. He needed a British passport.'

To her consternation, Jill cracked a wide, knowing smile. 'You're talking about that gorgeous hunk who came in here looking for you a couple of weeks ago? Oh, Sabrina! You dark horse!'

'Before you leave tonight, I'll give you my new home telephone number, just in case you ever need to reach me there.' Heaving another large ring-binder onto her lap, Sabrina pushed her hair out of her eyes and mentally made a note to take more time with her appearance tomorrow. This morning she'd woken in a strange house with unfamiliar voices and unfamiliar sounds and had lain in bed feeling dazed at what she'd done. In a bid to give the family space and not get in the way, she'd hurriedly washed and dressed and raced out of the house without so much as a cup of coffee. Then she'd spent half an hour in one of those popular coffee chains, nursing a frothy cappuccino and feeling as if she'd burst into tears if someone so much as glanced at her the wrong way. Had Javier been surprised that she'd left for work so early? Or was he too concerned about his own activities once he'd delivered Angelina safely to school? He'd explained to Sabrina that he took the child in the morning and Rosie picked her up at three-thirty. And what did they do about dinner? Should Sabrina get something for herself on the way home, just in case she worked late?

A heartfelt sigh escaped her and she took a moment to absorb the fluttery feeling in her stomach. There was so much she didn't know. So much they hadn't had a chance to discuss.

'I'm sure *I* wouldn't be looking half so glum if I'd just got married to someone as seriously sexy as him.'

'Please, Jill.' Pursing her lips, Sabrina picked up the phone. 'Can we just get on? I really don't feel like discussing this right now if you don't mind.'

'All right, but don't think you're getting off as lightly as all that. And I'm seriously miffed you didn't even have a hen night.'

Rolling her eyes, Sabrina put down the receiver without making her phone call. 'I told you, it wasn't like that. We only got married to—'

The little bell over the door jingled and both women glanced up to see Javier D'Alessandro step inside. He acknowledged Jill's presence with a brief nod of his head but his gaze—deep, dark and intense—gravitated almost immediately to Sabrina. Her anxiety increased tenfold.

'Hi. This is a surprise.' Feeling Jill's scrutiny beside her, Sabrina strove to keep her voice light, but everything inside her was going crazy at just the sight of the man. He looked like the successful young entrepreneur he was in his effortlessly elegant suit and expensive overcoat, his sexy masculine fragrance leaving an indelible presence on the room.

'A pleasant one, I hope?'

Sabrina dipped her head. 'Of course. What can I do for you? Did Angelina get off to school all right?'

'She's fine. You left without having breakfast, without joining us.' Was that reproach in his voice?

'I'm sorry, I...' She turned and looked at Jill, who clearly had forgotten why she was there. 'Don't you have some clients to ring this morning, Jill? I'm just going to take Mr D'Alessandro...' Flushing, she realised her mistake and stood up in a rush. 'We just need to have a talk. If there are any calls for me, please tell them I'll call back just as soon as I can.'

In the back room, she busied herself putting the kettle on to boil and sorting out the makings of tea and coffee. For several seconds Javier just watched her, his brain working overtime with the effort to fathom her out. Was she regretting marrying him? Was she too unhappy and uncomfortable in Michael's house? As soon as he could look for somewhere for them all to move to, he would. But he still wanted to know why she'd felt the need to escape so early this morning, without so much as even bidding them goodbye. On the way to school Angelina had asked curiously if they had had a row.

'Sabrina.'

She jumped at the sound of his voice, spilling a little of the hot water from the kettle onto her hand. 'Ouch!'

'Let me see.' Before she had a chance to guess his next move he was at her side, taking her throbbing hand into his, turning it over for examination then leading her to the old-fashioned sink by the back wall and turning on the cold tap. The water barely cooled her heated skin, she was so unravelled by his touch. Feeling all her blood roar in her ears, Sabrina tried to pull her hand free, and when she managed it and turned off the tap Javier put one hand on his hip and rubbed at his temple as if he had a severe headache.

'Have I offended you in some way, Sabrina? Because if I have I wish you would tell me.' She smelled so good, he was thinking. Flowers and honey with a subtle undertone of musk. A warm, sexy fragrance that was making him feel things he had no business feeling towards a woman who had only agreed to marry him because of a business arrangement. Her soft, dewy complexion was highlighted by two bright spots of pink and her silky honey-brown hair was slowly working its way loose from her tortoiseshell comb. And her eyes… *Dios!* Her eyes! They were so blue he thought he could drown in them—like an ocean.

'You haven't offended me, Javier. Why would you think that?'

'Why did you run away this morning?'

'Run away?' What a curious thing to accuse her of, even if it happened to be true.

'We wanted you to join us for breakfast, Angelina and I. We all need to get to know each other better, yes?'

'I didn't know what you expected. I didn't want to intrude,' Sabrina confessed, flushing again.

'Intrude? How could that be when I asked you to come and live with us? I do not expect you to hide yourself away or creep around the house like a mouse! It is your home as well as ours.'

'Perhaps we need to talk about some ground rules. It's an unusual situation, Javier; right now I don't know how to play it.'

'Just be yourself, Sabrina. If we all just try and relax it might make things easier for all of us. Angelina will come round, given time. It is early days yet. Already she has expressed interest in you.'

'She has?'

'She told me you had a much better figure than my

ex-girlfriend.' He chuckled and the sound made goosebumps chase across her skin.

'Christina.' She bit her lip.

His eyes seemed to grow even darker. 'She told you about Christina?'

'Just in passing. Do you mind?'

'No. I don't mind. I have barely even given the woman a thought, so much has happened lately.'

What did that mean? Sabrina worried. Was he still in love with her?

'And Angelina is right. You *do* have a nicer figure than Christina.' Javier smiled and the impact of that simple gesture caused all sorts of complications in Sabrina's heart. Not least—how was she going to live with a man who bothered her more than she cared to acknowledge? Her husband who wasn't really a husband at all.

'I'll make us some coffee. Or perhaps you'd prefer tea?'

'Coffee is fine, thank you.' To Sabrina's surprise he took off his overcoat and laid it over the back of an old office chair. 'When you have made the coffee I thought we could begin work.'

'What do you mean?' She stopped spooning coffee grounds into a mug and spun round to face him.

'It is time I started to fulfil my part of our agreement,' he said smoothly, 'to help you with your business. If we can spend today going over your books et cetera, then tonight I will devote some time to working out modernisation costs. The sooner we start, the better—yes?'

'Javier, you don't have to do this.'

'What?' He was frowning, dark eyes suddenly troubled.

'If you want to give me some advice I'll accept it gratefully but anything else…' She shrugged and went back to making the coffee. 'I was happy to do what I did for you. I don't need repayment. Honestly.'

If someone had dropped a brick on his head right then, Javier couldn't have been more stunned. Sliding his hands into the pockets of his tailored black trousers, he shook his head. 'You would do this thing for me…for nothing?'

'Lending me your expertise and your business knowledge would be more than enough payment.' Blushing, Sabrina added a little milk to her own drink and stirred it. 'As for modernisation, I'll find the money from another source. I haven't given up yet.' *Nor will I.*

His tanned brow furrowing, Javier wasn't appeased. 'I do not want you to find the money from another source. We have an agreement. An agreement I intend to fulfil.'

'All right,' Sabrina conceded reluctantly, wondering what it would mean to be under such an obligation to a man like Javier D'Alessandro. And, although she'd married him and fulfilled her own part of the agreement—what exactly would marriage to him entail? In the middle of all this was a sad, hurting eleven-year-old girl who would need care and attention from both of them. If Sabrina's heart got involved, what then? Weren't the lines of their so-called 'agreement' going to get dangerously blurred?

'I'll agree to your financial help as well—but only

if we work out an instalment plan for me to pay you back.'

'No.'

'Yes. I insist.'

'You are a stubborn woman, you know that?'

'Some people call it tenacious. I'm used to facing mountains and finding a way over them.' Wincing, she mentally pushed aside the sudden cloak of weariness that descended on her shoulders. She'd always worked hard. She didn't know any other way. Was it because from a young age she'd always felt she had something to prove? Ellie was their parents' blue-eyed girl. Whatever she did was praised to the skies. And when Ellie had given up her phenomenally well-paid City job to stay at home and become a full-time wife and mother, well…her parents were ecstatic at her 'selflessness.'

'I did what I did to help you out, Javier. I don't regret it.'

She meant it. Dear God, the woman barely knew him or Angelina and yet she had already done so much to alleviate their predicament. Now she was telling him that if she allowed him to help her, she insisted on paying him back. Such nobility was a rare commodity indeed in the circles he had moved in. Life in the fast lane had not exactly paved the way for lasting friendships with the kind of friends who would immediately help you out if you were in trouble or even pay you back if they borrowed money. His mother would bless the ground Sabrina Kendricks walked on, he realised—the thought making him warm. Or should he say Sabrina *D'Alessandro*?

Marriage of convenience or not—this charming, generous woman was his wife now.

'We are going to turn East-West Travel into a thriving modern business,' he declared, suddenly fired up at the thought. Sabrina couldn't yet know he was a man who thrived on a challenge. He didn't give up easily—not even on so-called lost causes. She would discover that about him.

'I notice your other employee is not here today.'

'You mean Robbie. He's on a couple of days' leave.'

'Then I may use his computer?'

'Of course, but Javier—' her hand curled round his arm and they both reacted strongly at the contact, a flash of something Sabrina couldn't discern in Javier's dark Latin eyes and a leap in her own heart that made her words get caught in her throat '—you don't have to do this.'

Her hand dropped away, and to her shock Javier tilted her chin and smiled into her anxious blue gaze. 'That is where you are mistaken. It is a point of honour for me and I never go back on my word. Bring the coffee and we will get to work.'

Bring the coffee? Normally she would have bristled at such a chauvinistic-sounding command but for some reason today Sabrina didn't seem to be operating on her usual wavelength. As soon as Javier had walked through the door she'd been functioning on a different frequency and she got the feeling it was one she was going to have to get used to, whether she liked it or not.

CHAPTER FIVE

FOR two days Sabrina worked side by side with Javier, going through accounts, client lists and schedules, meticulously sifting through everything that would give him a good picture as to how East-West Travel was currently being run. She'd discovered that when his mind was on work his concentration was unequalled, and, apart from when it was necessary to ask pertinent questions, he kept his head down—barely acknowledging whatever else was going on around him. To Sabrina's irritation, in between dealing with customers, Jill had taken it upon herself to keep him furnished with regular offers of tea and coffee and even popped out to the most expensive deli in the high street to get him the sandwiches he asked for. It was obvious that he had acquired a fan in her colleague.

That first evening when she returned home on her own, Javier having left earlier to see Angelina, she'd arrived back at the house to find that they'd waited dinner for her. Angela Calder had returned to her own home in the Cotswolds, promising to be back in a week or two to see her grandchild, and Rosie had cooked a wonderfully fragrant lamb tagine for them. After Sabrina's initial hesitance at joining Angelina and Javier at the dinner table, she tucked into the food with relish. If they were a little light on conversation she didn't mind—it was the child the adults were concerned about. Angelina hardly ate a thing. In the end Javier suggested to Rosie that perhaps she could make some sandwiches and put them in the fridge, in case his niece wanted something later. Excusing herself from the table, Angelina disappeared into her bedroom and shut the door. Minutes later pop music rang out and Javier glanced at Sabrina with a faintly weary look and shrugged.

'She'll be all right,' she softly assured him, wishing she didn't feel so hopelessly inadequate to help. 'Perhaps I can ask if she'll let me see her CD collection later.'

'Why not,' Javier agreed, pouring them both a glass of wine. 'Right now all we can do is take one day at a time. By the way, have you rung your parents yet?'

'I was going to do it tonight' she replied, a pang of guilt stabbing through her. Truth to tell, she'd barely given the matter another thought—especially when her head was swimming with thoughts of work and the kind of improvements Javier was going to suggest.

His dark brows came together in slight disapproval. 'Please, Sabrina. Do not put it off any longer. Your parents should be informed.'

She sat back in her chair, her cheeks flushed. 'You make me sound about five years old.'

That elicited a rueful grin. 'Forgive me. I am just concerned they would find out by accident and that would not be good.'

'No. I see what you mean. Well…' She got to her feet and brushed back her hair with her hand. 'There's no time like the present, then, is there?'

Her announcement didn't go down well. Her

mother cried because 'after all this time she still hadn't seen her eldest daughter married' and her father interrogated her on just about everything to do with Javier. He could have had a job with Interpol, Sabrina reflected without humour. By the time she came off the phone, all Sabrina could face was a shower then bed, but she did fulfil her intention of dropping by Angelina's room and asking to see her music collection. After spending just over an hour with the little girl, listening to music, Angelina bade her goodnight but not before tentatively suggesting that Sabrina might like to listen to some more tracks the following night. Eagerly, Sabrina agreed and she went to bed feeling a little lighter than when she'd come off the phone to her parents.

The following evening after their meal, Sabrina was heading for her room and a shower when Javier waylaid her in the corridor. He'd taken off his tie and undid the first couple of buttons on his shirt, and Sabrina caught an intriguing glimpse of strongly corded neck muscles and a smattering of the dark hair that covered his chest. Heat invaded her limbs. 'Tomorrow we will visit your bank and deposit some funds for the modernisation programme,' he informed her without preamble, 'then we will have lunch together.'

'Lunch?' Her voice had turned unwittingly husky. Javier seemed to concentrate his dark gaze even more.

'There is a need to discuss how we are going to proceed.'

There was something inexplicably sensual about his almost formal use of the language—every word carefully considered.

'With modernising the business, you mean?' She was feeling somewhat overwhelmed at the idea that, with Javier's much-needed help, she was finally going to be able to realise her dreams for the company.

'That and other things.' He smiled. 'I will book somewhere.'

'I haven't yet thanked you for all you're doing.' She twirled a button on her blue linen jacket and felt the thread loosen. 'I can't tell you how much it means to me. It's been such a worry for so long…'

'It is a small thing compared to what you have done for me and Angelina,' he replied sincerely. 'And I am excited by it too. I think you will be amazed what can be achieved.'

'Anyway…' Glancing almost shyly up at him from beneath her honey-brown lashes, Sabrina wondered what had happened to the single-minded businesswoman who was so certain she neither wanted nor needed a man in her life. She was sure that even her mother would detect the difference in her since she'd met Javier D'Alessandro. Her hard edges had been somehow softened. In his presence she was discovering new aspects to herself all the time. Worrying. Especially when one day soon she'd have to walk away and maybe not even see him again. 'I'm going to take a shower.'

His reaction staggered her. Leaning back against the wall, his arms folded across that incredible chest, he smiled lazily. 'Let me know if you need my assistance.'

'What?' Her stomach fluttering crazily, Sabrina blushed like a schoolgirl.

'Scrubbing your back.' He smiled again. 'Relax, Sabrina. I am only teasing.'

Teasing or not, his suggestive tone had all but turned her bones to jelly. 'I knew that.' Hoping her face didn't reflect the turmoil that was churning her up inside, she turned to walk with as much dignity as she could muster down the corridor to her room.

Madre del Dios! Rubbing his hand across his forehead, Javier wasn't surprised to find that he was perspiring. The sexual charge he had received from his new wife simply by spending a few minutes in light conversation had completely thrown him. Her scent had been taunting him, the dimples at the corners of her lush mouth fascinating him beyond reason. If he had spent a minute longer with her he was almost certain he would have reached out to touch her in some way. That most definitely hadn't been part of his plan. Theirs was a paper marriage only—sexual favours weren't part of the package. Unfortunately he hadn't been able to transmit that fact to his body. Just the brief thought of Sabrina naked beneath the warm spray of a shower, soaping that shapely, sexy body, had heat rushing to his groin like fire. What was he supposed to do? He was a young, virile man with more energy than he sometimes knew what to do with and right now a hot, sweet tumble in bed with a beautiful, warm, willing woman was the only thing he craved. And not just *any* beautiful, willing woman either—it was Sabrina he wanted, rightly or wrongly. Cursing harshly beneath his breath, he turned towards his room to seek a shower of his own—a very icy cold shower that would drive away the suddenly rampant desire that was hijacking his body, before being confronted with the temptation of her smile again.

Ellie didn't mince her words. She flung into the room with Tallulah on her hip, her champagne-blonde hair dishevelled by the fierce wind outside and an expression like a storm cloud on her face. 'You must be out of your mind!' Dropping her bag onto a nearby chair, she ignored Jill and Robbie and stared angrily at Sabrina, who up until a moment ago had been concentrating on the screen in front of her.

'Nice to see you too, Ellie.' Scowling at the unwanted interruption, Sabrina started to get to her feet. 'Hello, Tally, are you going to give Auntie a kiss?' She reached out her arms for her niece and was foolishly hurt when Ellie didn't pass the baby to her as she normally would have done.

'I couldn't believe it when Mum told me you'd gone and got married to a perfect stranger! Have you completely taken leave of your senses, Sabrina Kendricks?'

'Let's have some privacy, shall we?' Sabrina put her hand beneath her sister's elbow and guided her reluctantly into the back room. Closing the door, she flicked her blue eyes angrily over her. 'How dare you just walk in here and start yelling at me? This is a professional business, in case you had forgotten. What if there'd been a room full of customers?'

'I don't give a—' She bit back the curse word and jiggled the baby, who had started to whimper. 'What do you know about this man? How do you know he isn't out to take you for every penny you have? Did you check him out before you married him? And why didn't you tell me you'd met someone?'

'Take me for every penny I have?' Sabrina's laugh was harsh. 'If only you knew the irony of that remark.'

'For God's sake, what were you thinking of?'

'Drop it, Ellie. I'm thirty-seven years old, damn it! I don't need your permission to live my life the way I choose. And if you knew Javier D'Alessandro you wouldn't have to ask me such questions.'

Ellie transferred the baby to her opposite hip and glared. 'But I don't know him, do I? That's the whole point! None of us do. I know I told you that you needed to date more but I didn't expect you to go and marry the first man who asks you!'

'You're making it sound ridiculous.'

'It *is* ridiculous! What's the matter, Sabrina? Did you suddenly get scared of growing older and not having a man in your life? If that was the case, why didn't you just join a dating agency rather than marry a complete stranger off the street?'

Hurt welled in Sabrina's chest. She knew it was because Ellie had inadvertently touched a nerve. Had she been scared about getting older and being alone? Maybe not consciously, but she couldn't pretend that the thought hadn't ever crossed her mind. However, she'd married Javier to help him get a British passport, so that he could stay and raise Angelina as his own. She didn't kid herself it was a real marriage. He was only thirty. One day he'd want to marry someone his own age and add to his family. God! She didn't even know if she was capable of having children.

Seeing the sudden strain on her sister's face, Ellie

shook her head in remorse. 'I'm sorry, sis. I've just been worried out of my mind since Mum told me. He—he hasn't tried anything, has he?'

'You mean, has he attempted to get me into bed?'

Ellie had the grace to flush. Tallulah smiled, her chubby, grinning face catching Sabrina on the raw.

'He's not interested in me that way. I explained to Mum it was purely a business arrangement.'

'I'll believe it when I see it. When can I meet him? What did you say his name was?'

'Javier.' Sabrina took a shaky breath. 'Come on Saturday if you like. Mum's got the address.'

'Saturday, then. Look after yourself, sis. You know where I am if you need me.'

'You seem…preoccupied today.'

Javier's voice broke into Sabrina's thoughts. Glancing down at her coffee, she picked up the spoon in the saucer and gave it a stir. The smart little restaurant in an exclusive Knightsbridge thoroughfare was full of deliciously mouthwatering smells, but she hadn't been able to do full justice to the wonderful pasta she had ordered.

'Do I?' She raised her shoulders in a slight shrug. 'I'm sorry. Understandably I've had a lot on my mind.'

'Are you happy with my suggestions for the business?'

'Of course. But Javier—so much money… I really am going to have to insist on paying you back, you know.' Richard Weedy would surely never dare to look down his nose at her again after the outrageous amount Javier had paid into her bank just an hour ago.

'You have already paid me back. We have an agreement and I am merely honouring my part. The matter is at an end. The money is yours to make the improvements we discussed and whatever else you want to do with it.'

'The matter is not at an end, Javier. I won't be easy in my mind until we work out some kind of repayment plan. I mean it!'

'It has become clear to me that you find it difficult to accept help of any kind, Sabrina. It is not so good to be too independent, I think.'

His stern tone made her bristle slightly. Her chin came up. 'We have a very different culture here, Javier. Women are encouraged to have their own careers, make their own lives, without men dictating what they do.'

A flash of anger crooked his mouth. '*Sí.* You think it an achievement to bypass marriage and family? You are setting yourself up for a very lonely existence, I think.'

'I've never been lonely in my life! I enjoy my work—the challenge, the achievement. It gives me all the stimulation I need.'

The tension between them grew. 'Forgive me, but I think you need more than that. Men and women were meant to be together in mutual partnership. It is not something to shy away from because you are frightened you will be surrendering your independence. A clever woman allows the man to think he has all the power, but really *she* is the one in control.'

'So how come you haven't got married until now?

Not forgetting that this is just a temporary arrangement. No doubt you've been pursuing your own career with a vengeance, otherwise how could you be so successful?' Her heart was beating a little too fast and she wished she'd never started this conversation. She didn't want his antagonism…she wanted something much more *dangerous* than that.

His hand reached for his tie and loosened it. With one arm resting on the table top he scooped some sugar into the little silver spoon in the sugar bowl and watched the grains slide gracefully back in. He did this twice more before speaking.

'I didn't consider marriage before because I had seen what can happen when you give your heart to someone. Divorce, bereavement… I didn't want to set myself up for so much pain.' A shadow stole across his handsome face. 'Perhaps I am a coward.'

Impossible. Swallowing hard, Sabrina slowly shook her head. 'I don't think a man who would risk asking a relatively strange woman to marry him so that he could get a passport to stay in the country and adopt his niece could ever be deemed a coward in any way. You *should* marry properly some day, Javier. You should marry someone your own age and have lots of children to give Angelina brothers and sisters. You would make a wonderful father.'

The conviction in her voice shook him to his innermost core. Pinning her with a darkly brooding gaze, he smiled briefly. 'We will see. Let us change the subject and talk about the business. Tomorrow I will start ordering the new equipment. You will be upside-down for a while in the office but I am sure your staff will be able to work around that.'

'They're as excited as me about it all.' As she felt another rush of gratitude, her blue eyes shone. 'And you don't mind giving us all a little training in the new programme?'

'It will be my pleasure.'

'You seem to know so much. I feel like such a dinosaur in comparison.'

'Stop putting yourself down.' With a small sigh, Javier considered her so intensely that every nerve she possessed snapped into full and immediate attention. 'You have fifteen years' experience of running a successful business. There is much you could teach me, I'm sure.'

Why did Sabrina get the feeling it wasn't just her business technique he was talking about? *Wishful thinking,* she concluded disparagingly. Thinking about her husband in bed was becoming an obsession. She gulped her coffee and returned the cup noisily to its elegant green and gold saucer.

'I had a visit from my sister yesterday—Ellie. I invited her to the house on Saturday to meet you. Was that all right?'

'That is good, yes.' His lips parted, showing those perfect white teeth, and for a long moment Sabrina just basked in the pleasure of his smile.

'I hope you still think it's good after she's gone. I'm afraid my sister isn't one for standing on ceremony. Neither does she pull her punches.'

Javier frowned.

'She says exactly what she thinks,' Sabrina explained. 'I just thought I'd better warn you.'

'No doubt it is because she cares about you.' Signalling the young waitress for more coffee, he stayed silent while she refilled both their cups. When she'd gone, he leant forward towards Sabrina and snagged her hand. His touch electrified her. All she heard was the wave-like pounding of her blood in her ears. 'It is good to have family who care.'

'The way you do for Angelina.'

'Sí.' He released her hand to sit back in his chair and Sabrina didn't miss the flash of concern his dark eyes exhibited. 'I have already talked to the authorities concerned about adoption. I have been advised there should be no problem. It is a big relief, yes?'

'Yes, it must be. That little girl deserves something good to happen. She seemed a little brighter yesterday, don't you think?'

'I am glad you noticed. I thought so too. This evening I thought we might all go out for the evening—to the movies perhaps?'

'Javier, I...'

'What is it, Sabrina?'

'We need to talk about us...about—about our arrangement.'

'You are unhappy about something?'

'No! But...where do we draw the line exactly? I mean, I want to help you with Angelina but this marriage of ours isn't real, is it? And I—'

'Isn't real?' He was scowling heavily, immediately alert. 'We said our vows in front of the proper authorities, no? We signed the papers. Of course this marriage is real.'

'You know very well what I mean.' She rubbed the side of her temple and wondered why the room suddenly felt so unbearably hot. 'We agreed it's a formality—a business arrangement. That understood, I can't be so involved in your life. There have to be lines we absolutely don't cross. Do you see what I'm getting at?'

'You do not like spending time with me and Angelina?'

Mortified, Sabrina rushed to reassure him. Without thought she automatically reached out for his hand, covering those fascinating brown fingers with her own pale ones. Heat immediately made its presence felt but she couldn't let go. 'How could you ever think that? I care about you both.'

Her words warmed Javier like a deep draught of brandy stealing into his blood and he couldn't help but smile. 'We are fine as we are, Sabrina—wouldn't you say? As far as I can see, nothing has to be changed.'

Oh, this was getting complicated. Biting her lip, Sabrina slid her hand away from his. She stared down into her coffee, feeling as though all the control she'd assumed over her life for the past fifteen years was slowly but surely slipping away.

'I will order you some dessert. You hardly ate any of your lunch.' Before she could stop him, Javier had summoned the pretty young waitress and ordered some rich-sounding sweet that Sabrina knew under normal circumstances she'd be sorely tempted by. However, her current circumstances weren't normal at all and the pudding would no doubt go to waste.

'You shouldn't have done that.'

'You need to eat. In my country, men look after their women.' He said it so matter-of-factly that Sabrina didn't know whether to hit him with something or simply submit to the inevitable. She'd been taking care of herself for so long now that the mere concept of a man assuming any kind of responsibility for her welfare was completely alien.

'We're back to that again, are we? Have you even heard of feminism in Argentina?' she retorted, rattled.

In return he gave her one of those slow, deeply sexy smiles that made her insides dissolve like melting sugar. 'Some of it we younger men embrace—some we don't.'

'I don't think I should get into this argument.' Her face flushed, blue eyes resentful, she sank back into her chair with a sigh and folded her arms across her chest.

'You think I mind you arguing with me? I like a woman who knows her own mind. I have no problem with you expressing your views, Sabrina. Even if I don't happen to agree…'

So much for establishing where we stand. Staring down at the incredible chocolate concoction the waitress placed in front of her, Sabrina picked up her spoon and defiantly tucked in.

Javier paused outside his niece's door. Was that laughter he had heard or had his foolish, hopeful heart just imagined it? He knocked briefly at the door and his shoulders automatically tightened as Angelina called out, 'Come in, Uncle.'

The sight that met his eyes had him staring in stunned disbelief. CDs and tapes spread out on the floor all around them, Angelina and Sabrina were lying front down on the carpet, propped up on their elbows, sifting through discs like two giggling schoolgirls. Although with Sabrina dressed in tight denims and a little pink T-shirt that was riding above her waist, her long hair loose down her back, she was most definitely all grown up. Javier's breathing felt suddenly laboured. 'What's going on?' he asked lightly, feeling oddly excluded.

'We're just listening to some music and talking about girl stuff.' Angelina's small shoulders shrugged as if it should be perfectly obvious. 'Sabrina said that her sister got my favourite singer's autograph at a concert and she's going to ask her on Saturday if I could have it.'

'That's nice.' Moving to the bed with its bright pink Barbie duvet, Javier sat down, his gaze helplessly gravitating to Sabrina's long, slim legs in soft, hugging denim and the sweet curve of her sexy rear end.

'Did you want something, Javier?' she asked him, smiling. Was it his fevered imagination or was there a more intimate invitation in that smile of hers?

'Yes, Uncle, because if you don't, we'd really like some privacy—wouldn't we, Sabrina?'

'I was just going to offer you both a drink of some kind. How about some fruit juice or a glass of milk, Angelina?' Rising to his feet, he dug his hands into his trouser pockets, irked that he suddenly felt superfluous to the needs of the women in his life.

'Juice is fine, Uncle. How about you, Sabrina?'

'Sure. Thanks.'

'OK. See you in a minute.'

There was a wildlife documentary on the TV about tigers in India he'd wanted to see but, once settled in the big luxurious armchair, the remote control at his elbow, Javier couldn't work up an interest. Not when

Angelina had actually bid him goodnight with a smile on her face for the first time in weeks and Sabrina was taking a shower. Did the woman tell him she was going to take a shower just to taunt him? He shifted against the cushions at his back, cursing softly at the discomfort of having his blood head south with a vengeance.

He flicked off the TV and raked his fingers irritably through his hair. Almost of their own volition his feet took him out of the room, down the thickly carpeted corridor to what was now Sabrina's room. He rapped briefly on the door.

He heard movement from within, the sound of something thunking to the floor and her muttered curse. His heart beat a little faster.

'Hi.' Her face pink from the shower, dressed in a thick white towelling robe and with her long hair scooped up into a loose topknot, she looked deliciously feminine and warm. Javier knew he was playing with fire. *This isn't part of the plan,* he told himself. *I don't want to care about this woman. I don't want to desire her the way I do…*

'Is everything all right?' he asked after a long moment spent just gazing at her as a starving man gazed at a banquet.

'You're too late if you've come to scrub my back,' came her rejoinder, blue eyes issuing a challenge that hit him square in the solar plexus.

'My bad luck, I guess.' As he stepped into the room, Sabrina heard the soft 'snick' of the door closing behind him with a thundering heart.

CHAPTER SIX

'WHAT are you doing?' Her hands went to her robe, fingering the soft collar, absently stroking the material. Seeing the small pulse beat at the side of his temple, she got the strangest sensation that she'd been waiting all her life for his answer.

'Looking at you,' he replied. 'Do you mind?'

Sabrina had heard of being stripped naked by a man's eyes, but her husband was way ahead. He was shamelessly making love to her with that slumberous dark gaze of his, heating her blood with a potent mixture of fire and pure masculine chemistry, making her skin prickle with the sensation of being physically touched in the most intimately erotic way. Inside her robe her nipples peaked, the intense, aching throb bordering on pain. Moisture spread between the juncture of her thighs as her knees literally started to shake.

'You should go.' Finding her voice, she silently acknowledged it had no real conviction. How could it when she craved him the way parched land needed rain?

'We never kissed when we exchanged vows.' He took a step nearer until her startled gaze was in direct line with the second white button on his shirt. The exposed V of his skin appeared very bronze and all the more appealing because of it. The heat they were engendering between them turned up the temperature in the room another notch.

'I would very much like to remedy that, Sabrina.'

When his hands settled possessively around her upper arms, his breath drifting feather-light touches across her face, Sabrina focused on his mouth. That perfect, strong impression of everything that was Javier D'Alessandro—courage, honour, strength and enough sizzling personal attraction to melt all the ice in a glacier.

When that same mouth slanted possessively across hers, she leaned into his kiss as if the decision had been totally taken out of her hands and she might as well bow to the inevitable. With a husky sound of hungry need, she willingly opened to the invasion of his tongue, welcoming his hotly intimate exploration as if it was the Christmas gift she'd always dreamed of but never had. Her fingers curled into the hard, iron strength of his shoulders beneath the silkiness of his shirt, even as he hauled her urgently against the granite wall of muscle and sinew that was his chest. Deepening the kiss until he could hear the wild roar of his own blood in his ears, his heart thumping with all the force of a blacksmith's hammer, Javier told himself he had no right to hold her like this, to demand so much when she had already saved his life by marrying him. But when reason was weighted against pure, raging desire, it made a poor persuader. The sweet, fresh pine scent of her shampoo, her warm, giving body still glowing from her shower making seductive little asides into his senses, Javier's hands moved from her arms to slide up her back, pressing her closer still. Every one of her delicious feminine curves melded with the harder lean contours of his own proudly male body and he was heavily, almost painfully aroused.

With great reluctance Sabrina forced herself to come to her senses. Her small, elegant hands sliding down his shirt, she pushed against him, staring up at him with blue eyes that were dark with longing and regret. She shouldn't be doing this. *They* shouldn't be doing this.

Javier let loose a muffled curse in Spanish. *'Madre del Dios!'*

'We can't. This wasn't part of our agreement.' She shot him a nervous smile.

'No.' Stepping away, ostensibly to put temptation out of reach, he reluctantly agreed. Then, changing his mind, he shook his head, hands dropping angrily to his hips. 'Is it wrong that I should desire you? I know we have an agreement but I am a living, breathing man with hot blood running through my veins! Am I supposed not to notice when you smile at me as if you're pleased to see me, or tell me that you're going to take a shower with an invitation in your eyes? I cannot pretend not to want you, Sabrina. It would be denying my own nature.'

'If we are to see this thing through then you have to! Six months down the line, when Angelina's adoption comes through and we sign the divorce papers, I'll be leaving to take up where I left off, Javier, and so will you. We have to be sensible.'

'Sensible?' Frustration crawling through his skin, Javier glared at her. 'You do not know what you ask. Is the business all you think of? You must have ice in your veins, woman!' Without another word, he turned and exited the room, slamming the door behind him.

* * *

'Good morning, Angelina. What have you got lined up at school today? Something nice, I hope.' Sweeping into the kitchen, dressed in a navy-blue linen suit and carrying her briefcase, Sabrina paused at the work-top to pour a cup of coffee from the percolator, then brought it to the table to join the little girl dressed in her grey and green uniform, her black hair in two neat braids. Angelina acknowledged Sabrina's presence with a slight dip of her head. Immediately sensing something amiss, Sabrina slid her hand across the child's.

'What's the matter, darling? Not feeling well this morning?'

She shook her head without saying a word. The silence was followed by two wet streaks tracking slowly down her pretty face. Sabrina's heart squeezed tightly. Without further ado, she cradled Angelina's head against her chest, stroking down the silky, soft hair, murmuring any words of comfort that came to mind. With a shudder, the little girl leaned deeper into Sabrina's jacket, her hand reaching out to clutch hers. The wave of love that surged through her at that trusting little touch made her eyes sting with tears.

'Oh, sweetheart. I know you're hurting but it will get better in time, I promise. You're being so brave, so brave.'

'Angelina, *mi angel*, what is wrong?' Suddenly Javier was there. Handsome and concerned, he dropped to his haunches beside them, rubbing Angelina's hunched back with firm, soothing strokes, his devastatingly dark gaze meeting Sabrina's, frowning at the tears he saw there.

'I think she's having a bad day,' she explained gently. 'I'll stay with her for a while. I don't have to rush.'

'Would you like that, Angelina? Would you like Sabrina to stay with you?'

The child sniffed and nodded.

'*Te amo.* Everything will be all right.' Planting a kiss at the side of her cheek, Javier smiled tenderly.

'There's some coffee in the pot,' Sabrina told him. 'Rosie must be around somewhere if you want breakfast.'

'She is just drying her hair.' Her small fist scrubbing at her eyes, Angelina hiccuped then leant her head back against Sabrina's chest. Noticing the small, trusting gesture with a thump in his chest, Javier got to his feet, gave Sabrina's shoulder a squeeze, then went across the room to pour himself some coffee.

'Have you eaten?' He directed his question to the both of them.

'I had some cornflakes, Uncle. I don't want anything else.'

'As long as you ate something, *mi querida.* We have to take great care of you. What about you, Sabrina? Can I get you some toast or cereal?'

'I don't usually have breakfast in the morning.'

'Why not?'

'I don't usually have the time.' She was drying Angelina's tears with the pad of her thumb, smiling into the sad little face, still holding her.

Again Javier felt his heart turn over. Was it only last night he had accused this woman of having ice in her veins? Because he had been burning up for her he had let his frustration boil over into an insult when she rejected him—an insult that he deeply regretted. Watching her now with his niece, her beautiful, candid blue eyes too bright, he concluded that his new wife was a natural mother. It was just a shame she didn't know it. 'You should make time,' he admonished, wishing his voice wasn't quite so stern because Sabrina threw him a bewildered look that pricked at his conscience badly. He would make it up to her, he promised himself. Later on today he would go out and buy her a gift of some kind—one for Angelina too. It would, he decided, give him the greatest pleasure to spoil them both a little.

When Sabrina still wasn't home at ten-thirty that same evening, Javier paced the living-room for a further five minutes before retracing his steps to the kitchen to stare at the note that Rosie had scribbled earlier and left for him propped up by the sugar basin: 'Sabrina rang. Said she's going out for a drink with a colleague and not to wait dinner.' Angelina was staying the night at a friend's house. Julie's parents had been good friends with Michael and had been pressing him for a while now to let Angelina come and stay. His niece had been happy to go and so Javier had raised no objections. He understood life had to go on and he wasn't about to curtail even the smallest pleasure if it made the child feel good. But where was Sabrina and what was keeping her? Who was this colleague she'd gone out with? Jill, or Robbie? He scowled at the thought of the young man who worked with her. He'd seen the admiring way he looked at Sabrina sometimes and it made Javier naturally a little cool towards him.

Switching on the radio, he flicked through the stations for something that wouldn't bite on his nerves. As the soothing strains of harp strings filled the room, he turned up the volume a little then poured himself a brandy. Remembering a stack of Spanish magazines he'd bought from the newsagents in Harrods, he returned to the living-room to fetch them, bringing them back to the large pine table in the kitchen. Sipping his brandy, he immersed himself in an article about the compelling virtues of the latest Italian sports car, smiling wryly to himself when he thought about the three similar models he had in his garage at home in Buenos Aires. Once upon a time they'd been his pride and joy. Now they did nothing for him. He would have to ring his cousin Enrique and tell him to take them for a spin.

It was ten minutes past midnight when he heard Sabrina's key in the door. Staring at his long empty brandy glass, the strains of a violin concerto playing softly in the background, Javier waited for her to come and find him. To tell the truth, he needed the extra time to compose his anger. What was she thinking, staying out this late? A woman alone? He hoped her colleague, whoever it was, had either seen her home or put her safely into a taxi.

'Hello. I didn't expect you to still be up.' She put her bag on a chair, kicked off her shoes and undid her jacket. Her honey-brown hair was drifting loose from its clip and there were faint shadows beneath her amazing eyes. Drumming his fingers on the table,

Javier fought the sudden wave of desire that engulfed him.

'Did you think I would go to bed knowing you were still out?'

'Please don't take that high-handed, superior male tone with me. I've had a long day and I'm not in the mood.' Even as she gave vent to the need to reassert her position, Sabrina sensed the tension coil in the man seated just a foot away from where she stood. She threw him a brief glance from beneath her golden-brown lashes, and a prickle of heat radiated all the way down her spine at the sight of him. He was so blatantly, unashamedly male, she thought. With his darkly smouldering good looks, he might have been one of those very conquistadores she had fantasised about. His sleek, midnight hair sexily mussed by impatient, perhaps angry fingers, a faint shadow of beard studding his lean, hard jaw, long, tautly muscled legs in black jeans stretched out in front of him, he was a force to be reckoned with.

'Dios!' The noise of his chair scraping violently against the smooth tiles of the floor had all Sabrina's nerves jumping in fright. 'I spend the whole evening worrying about you and all you do is give me this—this ''attitude'' in return!'

'I didn't ask you to worry about me. *That* wasn't part of our agreement either!'

'Who were you with tonight? Was it Robbie?'

Sabrina told herself she must be imagining his jealous, possessive tone. With her heart rioting inside her chest, she levelled her best glare. 'I don't believe you asked me that. It's none of your damn business who

I go out with, quite frankly. And I think you're taking this whole marriage thing a bit too far!'

Javier saw red. All of a sudden he wanted to show her that as far as he was concerned he wasn't taking it far enough. With enough sexual sparks between them to set the whole street alight, he was tired of pretending he didn't want her.

Taken aback by the hungry flare in his gaze, Sabrina stood rooted to the spot as he advanced, not quite believing what was happening when he pulled her roughly into his arms then crushed her mouth savagely beneath his. All her senses drowning and melting in his heat, at first she started to fight him—terrified of what she was feeling. Never in her whole life had she been swept away by such uncontrollable sensations of lust and longing. Within seconds his devastatingly sensual assault on her mouth was coaxing her into melting submission. She was opening to him, taking as much as she was giving, emitting raw little pleas for more as her hands wound round his neck, her fingers biting into his shoulders as he ground his pelvis into hers. His hands cupping her bottom through the silky linen of her skirt, he dragged the material upwards, running his palms up the backs of her thighs, pulling her in even tighter to his hips. Bending his head, he settled his mouth in the smooth, silky juncture between her nape and her shoulder, kissing her deeply until she felt the hot sting of his teeth in her flesh.

'Javier, please!' She was coming undone badly, past the point of no return, her hair tumbling loose onto her shoulders, her blue eyes a sea of stormy passion. A million miles away from the cool, focused businesswoman she had always striven to be. Javier lifted his head, touched his fingers to her moist, plundered mouth, uttered something husky and indecipherable in Spanish then said clearly, 'We should be in bed, *sí*?'

Trembling as though she would never stop, Sabrina knew she was beyond any pretence about the subject. '*Sí,*' she replied softly.

Above her in the semi-darkness, the breadth of Javier's magnificent shoulders thrillingly outlined in the shadows, he moved up her body, his long, hard-muscled limbs tangling with hers, the faint, spellbinding drift of his aftershave mingling with his elemental male heat, the die well and truly cast to ensure her complete and utter surrender. Sabrina arched her back, pulled him down towards her, drove her fingers through the short, silky strands of his ebony hair, hungrily sought his mouth with her lips—hard, urgent—then broke free, her breathing ragged and her heart wild. 'This can only happen once, Javier. After tonight it can't happen again. We have to be sensible. Ohh…' He stole her breath as he ran his hand across her hip, then trailed it deliberately down to the sweet dark cavern of her most intimate place. Pushing her slender, silken thighs apart, he introduced his fingers, those clever, sensitive fingers, sliding them in and out, daring deeper until she grabbed at his shoulders, urging him upwards, desperately seeking his mouth on hers once again.

He made her wait. He made her ride him slowly, then slid up to capture her breast in the seductive heat of his mouth, his tongue teasing and laving her burgeoning nipple, then nipping with his teeth. Sabrina bit back the sharp pleasure-pain, her fingers grabbing for the sheets to hold on as wave after wave of delicious capitulation shuddered through her.

Breathing hard, she stared up at him in wonder, seeking out those strong, mesmerising features of his in the shadows, biting her lip when he withdrew his hand to place his sex at her entrance, then, slowly but firmly, inserted himself deep inside her. Within seconds her ardour rose to meet his. Weaving her fingers through his hair, she opened to his deeply intimate kiss, then lifted her hips to meet the driving insistence of his as he filled her.

'Mi esposa hermosa,' he breathed raggedly against her ear and, although Sabrina didn't know what the words meant, her heart thrilled to hear them just the same.

His own heart beating high and wild, Javier took her hard and fast, his need to possess, to spill his seed in the deep, hot centre of her most feminine core completely taking him over so that every feeling, every emotion, every hungry, impossible hope in his soul played a vital part in his final destination. When he sensed the moment arrive, a cry burst from his throat, mingling with the raw, husky sound of his name on Sabrina's lips as her own journey reached its zenith. Then he fell against her, his mouth against her nape, breathing in her scent and her womanliness, feeling more satisfied and more alive than he had felt in months.

Carefully withdrawing from her body, he raised his head, staring down at her in the dimly lit glow, gently smoothing back her hair and tracing the exquisite line of her jaw with his finger, so that he could focus on her eyes. 'You are all right?' he asked, concerned. Perhaps he had been a little rough? Passion had overwhelmed him and her skin was so soft—easily bruised, no doubt…as tender as a baby's. The thought gave him pain.

'I'm more than "all right," Javier. That was wonderful.'

Her words warmed him all the way through. Almost of its own volition his knee started to manoeuvre her thighs apart. In a few more seconds he would be hard and ready for her again. His skin grew hot at the idea. This time he would take things more slowly, find out what gave her pleasure and make them both a little crazy.

'But it doesn't mean it's going to be a regular occurrence.' Her voice shook a little as Javier grazed his lips at the side of her mouth. 'We have Angelina to think about. We can't risk getting so involved. It's best if we keep things as—as professional as possible.'

Her words fell on deaf ears. Already Javier was positioning himself at her centre, pushing inside her with his satin hard length, making her ache for him all over again.

'Javier!' But her plea for understanding quickly turned into a plea for more of what he was presently delivering, and with a breathless little sigh she wound her arms tightly round his neck and raised her head for his kiss…

Stirring her coffee for the umpteenth time, Sabrina sat at the big pine table in the warm kitchen, staring at the lavishly wrapped gift in front of her as though it were a bomb about to detonate. Its shiny gold paper was topped off with a gorgeous white satin ribbon—also threaded with gold—fashioned into a huge bow, and next to the package was a little card with her name on it, simply signed 'Javier.' He'd told her this morning that he was taking Angelina to her usual Saturday-morning dance class and that he would be back to join her for breakfast.

Glancing at the clock, Sabrina saw that it was a little after nine. She would have to make sure she was showered and dressed before he returned because it surely wasn't a good idea to be sitting around in her dressing gown, considering the highly explosive situation that had now manifested between them. All night they had barely been able to keep their hands off one another. Sabrina had never known a more voracious or experienced lover. Everything they said about hot Latin lovers was true—even if it was a cliché. The man had magic oozing from his fingertips, not to mention more intimate places, and Sabrina's tender skin this morning was more than proof of that. Pulling aside her gown, she bit her lip at the sight of the small pink abrasions on the insides of her thighs. It made her tingle all over to remember where that particular little trail of his mouth had led.

Blowing out a guilty breath, she fanned herself then took a deep gulp of strong black coffee. What had possessed her to be so wild and free with her favours? What on earth had she been thinking of? The fact was, she hadn't been thinking at all. If she'd applied thinking to the situation she wouldn't be in the quandary she was in now. They might have enjoyed being intimate together but Javier wasn't looking to make this marriage real and Sabrina wasn't in the market for a man in her life—at least, not permanently. What needed to take precedence right now was what was happening to her business—the business she'd shed blood, sweat and tears over for the past fifteen years. She wasn't about to throw it all away just because she'd suddenly become enamoured with a man—a very generous, good-looking and sexy man.

'Oh, for goodness' sake, open it. It's not going to bite you!' With an exasperated sigh, Sabrina begin to tear at the wrapping paper, pulling it off in large swathes, her heart racing a little when she saw the smooth silver box inside. Lifting the lid, she stared down at the oyster-coloured satin in disbelief. *He'd bought her lingerie?* Running her fingertips across the sensuous material, she lifted out the exquisitely designed chemise with matching briefs and felt her cheeks burn red. No man had ever bought her anything so beautiful—or so intimate. For some inexplicable reason, tears sprang to her eyes. Then, impatiently dashing them away, Sabrina laid the silky items back against the soft tissue paper in their pretty box, put the lid back on, gathered up the torn gold wrapping paper, and carried the whole lot back into her room.

Minutes later, as piping hot water slooshed down her body from the shower, Sabrina knew that Javier D'Alessandro had got into her blood in a big, big way. It wouldn't be easy to walk away from that realisation when this 'marriage of convenience' of theirs finally came to an end—no matter how strong her resolve. But somehow she was going to have to find the strength and courage to achieve the impossible.

CHAPTER SEVEN

JAVIER was holding the baby and Tallulah was gazing back at him with adoring blue eyes. Beside her, Ellie elbowed Sabrina in the ribs.

'Ouch!'

'That man is dangerous with a capital "D",' said Ellie, dropping her voice low so that only her sister could hear, and grinned.

'Meaning?'

'Well, look at him. He's the answer to a woman's prayer, isn't he? Not only is he tall, dark and amazingly, knee-tremblingly handsome, but he's good with babies and children as well! No wonder you married him!'

Unfolding her arms from across her chest, Sabrina wished that the tight, breathless pain beneath her ribcage would go. Since she'd slept with Javier, every time she happened to glance at him for any reason at all, she felt it—not to mention the fluttery feeling in her stomach that seemed to accompany it. 'My reasons for marrying him aren't what you seem to think they are, I told you!' Exasperated, Sabrina walked to the living-room door. As her blue gaze swept the room, she paused to smile at Angelina, sitting cross-legged on the floor, helping William and Henry to dress a couple of worse-for-wear soldier figures. Her pretty face was a study in concentration and patience as the two little boys sat beside her, clearly enthralled by her willingness to play with them. In front of the fireplace, Javier was jiggling Tallulah up and down, making her laugh. 'I think I'll go and help Rosie in the kitchen,' she said lightly, catching his eye.

'Rosie is fine. Stay here and talk to our guests with me. Come.' He gestured for her to join him, his dark eyes teasing, almost mocking...*as if he could read her mind.* Inside her chest, her heart jumped at the thought. She was thinking about him, of course—of all the different delicious ways he had made love to her—and wondering when it might happen again. That caught her up short. It wasn't going to happen again. *It couldn't.*

'I can talk to Ellie any time,' she remarked breezily.

Ellie took immediate affront, tossing back her mane of blonde hair with a little huff. 'Thanks. I love you too. See what I have to put up with, Javier?' She lingered over his name as though it were some delicious sweetmeat. Sabrina could hardly believe what she was hearing. Was this the same woman who had torn her off a strip for being so ridiculous in agreeing to marry a man she barely knew? Even little Tallulah was mesmerised by him.

Sighing irritably, Sabrina reluctantly moved to stand next to her husband, her irritation briefly diverted by Tallulah's outrageously gummy grin. Automatically she held out her arms. 'Have you got a new admirer, Tally? Have you, darling?'

As Javier laughed and passed the baby carefully over to his wife, he whispered into Sabrina's ear, 'So has her auntie... Did you know that, sweet Sabrina?'

'Don't talk to me like that!'

'Why not?' His answering chuckle sent goosebumps scudding crazily all over her skin.

'So tell me, if you please, Ellie—is there anything about your job in the City that you miss?'

Relieved that he had diverted his attention to her sister, Sabrina buried her face in Tallulah's silky, soft blonde hair and breathed in her compelling baby scent like an injection of pure, sweet oxygen.

'Good lord, no!' Laughing, Ellie raised her small glass of sherry and took a sip. 'I know things can be mayhem at home when you've got little ones to look after and I know things don't always run to plan because you've got to allow for so much that's unexpected—but even so, I wouldn't change places for the world. I love being a mum. Phil loves me being a mum too, and quite frankly I wouldn't want some child-minder taking care of my kids just so that I could climb some dreary career ladder in the City! Been there, done that and it's not all it's cracked up to be, believe me.'

In her heart Sabrina knew her sister wasn't having a secret dig at her own choice to run a business, but even so her passionate renunciation of a career as opposed to having children made Sabrina feel slightly inadequate. Something her parents had a knack of making her feel too, if the truth was known. They absolutely doted on their three grandchildren and barely asked Sabrina anything about her day-to-day life apart from the stock, 'How is the business going?' and, 'Isn't it about time you found yourself a nice man and settled down?'

'You are clearly a natural mother.' Javier smiled approvingly and Sabrina was amazed to see the soft pink flush that highlighted her sister's beautiful cheekbones. Did every female between six months and one hundred years old fall under this man's spell? Clearly they did if the evidence she'd seen so far was anything to go on!

'Not *all* women are cut out to be mothers,' she commented defensively.

Immediately Javier's disturbing gaze settled thoughtfully on her face. 'How do you know if you never give yourself the chance to find out?'

'Sabrina thinks she's too old to have children.' Finishing her sherry, Ellie left the glass on a nearby bookshelf. 'Don't you, sis?'

'My mother was forty-two years old when she had me. It didn't prevent her from being a wonderful mother.' Javier was looking straight at Sabrina when he spoke and, riveted, she knew he was thinking about the time they'd spent together in bed making love. Was he wondering if he had perhaps made her pregnant? He hadn't used any protection and he hadn't even thought to ask if she was on the Pill. Which she wasn't—*Oh, God, how could she have been so stupid?*

'I'm not saying it's not possible to become pregnant in your late thirties or even early forties, I'm just saying that I don't think Sabrina sees herself in a maternal role. Do you, sis? She's much more interested in making a success of her business.'

'Why does that sound like a criticism?'

'I think you're being a little over-sensitive, Sabrina.'

'Do you? Well, then, you must be right. You usually are, aren't you?' Plonking a surprised baby

Tallulah into Javier's arms, she swept out of the room, hardly pausing for breath until she reached her bedroom and quietly shut the door behind her.

Her hands shaking, a little shudder of emotion sweeping down her spine, she moved across to the bed and dropped down onto the pale cream counterpane, shocked to find herself inexplicably in tears.

'Pull yourself together, for God's sake!' she scolded herself, then burst into a fresh bout of noisy weeping.

She didn't hear the person who quietly entered the room. It was only when she felt the soft pressure of that little hand on her back that Sabrina glanced up into a pair of sweet brown eyes full of concern.

'Are you all right, Sabrina? Uncle said I should come and find you.'

'I'm fine, Angelina, darling. I'm just being very silly.' Digging into her jeans pocket for a handkerchief, she loudly blew her nose, then smiled brightly at the little girl.

'I don't think you're being silly at all. You're crying. You must be upset about something. What is it, Sabrina?'

'Sweetheart, it's nothing. We've all just had to adapt to a lot of change lately. Sometimes even adults can feel overwhelmed.'

'I was worried when I heard you crying outside the door. Yesterday Uncle Javier was crying too.'

'He was?' Sabrina blinked in shock, her breath suspended. The thought of the strong, capable, sophisticated man who was now her husband reduced to real human tears was like being unexpectedly hit by one of those punch-bags in a gym.

'At first he pretended he wasn't, then he told me he was sad because my daddy had died and he missed him. They were good friends, you know. I told him it was OK to cry and miss my daddy because I do too. I miss him a lot.'

'Oh, sweetheart.' Her heart full, Sabrina pulled the child into her arms and kissed the top of her head. 'I am so sorry you're hurting so badly. It will get better, I promise. You won't forget but you'll be able to deal with it without feeling as if your whole world has come to an end.'

Seemingly satisfied with her reassurance, Angelina straightened and ventured a smile. 'I am glad you're here with me and my uncle. Perhaps you could make him feel better too?'

Out of the mouths of babes. Sabrina's stomach clenched tight. 'I'll try.' What she couldn't explain to the charming eleven-year-old was that her relationship with her gorgeous uncle was testing every single faculty she possessed to the limit—particularly the most threatening one of all: her heart. She hardly knew how to make herself feel better, let alone Javier. Now she had gone and slept with him she'd put herself under totally unnecessary duress in an already highly charged situation. Somehow she had to get it together and regroup, re-establish some of those ground rules Javier was so unenthusiastic about. It wasn't going to be easy, given her current vulnerability, but she would give it everything she had to restore her life to some semblance of normality.

'Rosie is laying the table for tea. I said I would go and help her. Will you come with me?'

Angelina was holding out her hand and suddenly

Sabrina felt mortally ashamed of being so obsessed with her own concerns when the sweet child in front of her was being so astoundingly brave, considering all that had happened to her. Checking beneath her eyes for tell-tale signs of wetness, Sabrina pushed herself to her feet, took Angelina's hand in hers then left the room to go and give Rosie a hand in the kitchen. As soon as Ellie and the children went home and Angelina was otherwise occupied, she resolved to speak to Javier in private and tell him the conclusion she'd reached. Even if he didn't like what she had to say, he would have to hear her out.

'I need to talk to you.'

Standing in the doorway to Michael's office, Sabrina stared at the back of Javier's dark head, at the breadth of those fine, strong shoulders, at the lean, tanned forearms exposed by the rolled-up sleeves of his perfectly white shirt as his fingers used the mouse to scroll up the screen in front of him.

Stretching his arms up high above his head, he swivelled in the chair and almost reduced her to a pile of smouldering embers on the carpet with the long, slow, lascivious look he had in his eyes.

She was only wearing jeans and an old blue and white shirt that she generally wore to do housework in, but she might as well have been standing there in the skimpiest of bikinis as far as the man in front of her was concerned.

'What is it?'

It was a simple enough question, though, annoyingly, the answer wasn't. With her heart knocking against her ribs, Sabrina took a deep breath and snaked her arms round her waist.

'I just wanted to sa—'

'Your sister was nice. I liked her.'

'Most men usually do.' She was thrown by the abrupt change of subject, and her response was out before she could check it. She flushed in embarrassment, knowing she sounded petty and jealous.

'I did not mean her looks—though of course she is pretty.' As he leaned back in his chair, his long legs stuck out in front of him just inches from where she stood, Javier's expression was thoughtful. 'I found her warm, approachable…capable. She is clearly a good mother.'

'Yes, she is.' Unfolding her arms, Sabrina impatiently pushed away a strand of hair that had drifted loose from her ponytail. 'She can do no wrong in my parents' eyes either.'

'That hurts you?'

Now, why did she have to go and tell him that? Nothing seemed to be going to plan today, absolutely nothing. She was like some damned sailing boat, rudderless and cast adrift on an unknown sea.

'I've got used to it. They never thought they'd have another child after me. Ellie is eight years my junior. When she came along I guess they were so happy at their unexpected gift that they simply doted on her. She was probably a much nicer child than me anyway. My mum always says I was too sulky and miserable.'

He laughed softly and all the hairs stood up on the back of her nape. 'You? Sulky? I cannot believe it.'

'Javier, I didn't come to make small talk. There is

a serious purpose to my wanting to talk to you.' She wouldn't let him distract her, she decided irritably. No matter how beguiling his smile or how wicked the look in those incredible black eyes.

'I am listening.' The light went out of his expression. He straightened in his chair and ran his hand through his hair.

'About…about what happened the other night.'

'In bed. *Sí.*'

Oh, boy. This was even harder than she'd suspected it might be. 'I was totally reckless, not thinking straight. I got—I got swept away.' Her blue eyes were so large and shimmering that Javier imagined he could dive right into them. Catching the drift of her scent on the air, he felt the muscles in his rock-hard stomach clench painfully. Ellie McDonald was pretty—but her sister, Sabrina, was beautiful.

'It happens. Passion has a life of its own.'

'You make it sound so simple.'

'It is. Perhaps we are not so repressed in my country in the way that the English are? You seem to want to apologise for everything…even desire.'

His comment completely unravelled her carefully worked-out bid for understanding. Trying to regroup, she shifted to her opposite hip, then folded her arms again across her shirt.

'Whatever. The point I'm trying to make is that it was a mistake. What we have here is a perfectly reasonable—though perhaps not commonplace—business arrangement. If we are both to come out of it intact we need to redefine our ground rules.'

'If we were in a boardroom right now I would be most impressed.' Getting restlessly to his feet, he pushed the black swivel chair right up to the desk then turned to face her. 'You do not have to try so hard to be the perfect businesswoman, Sabrina. Neither do you have to hide who you really are from me.'

'Hide?' Frowning, Sabrina desperately tried to keep her mind on track but it wasn't easy when she had six feet two inches of hard-muscled, devastatingly good-looking male staring back at her as if he wanted nothing better than to redefine ground rules of a completely different kind. The kind that had her pulse-rate rocketing off whatever scale it was measured on. 'I'm not trying to hide anything from you. All I'm trying to do is tell you that what happened between us was a mistake and shouldn't happen again. Please don't pretend you don't understand. I like you, Javier, and that's all to the good, considering our arrangement, but that's as far as it should go. I wanted to tell you that you should carry on as normal—go out with other women if you want to; I have no objection.'

'And that should make me glad?' His expression was forbidding. A muscle jumped in the side of his lean, bronzed cheek and Sabrina dropped her arms and twisted her hands together instead to still their sudden trembling.

'I'm not interested in whether it makes you glad or not!' *He was crying, Angelina had said. Missing Michael.* Probably feeling overwhelmed as well that, as a thirty-year-old successful single entrepreneur with no commitments but to himself, he now had to take on the awesome responsibilities of a child and live a completely different kind of life from the one he'd been used to living. One that no doubt included fast cars, pretty girls and the high-living pursuits of the rich and glamorous. 'All I know is that we need to get on with our own lives. I'm totally happy to help with Angelina, to be her friend if she wants me to—but, other than that, I can't get personally involved with you, Javier. I just can't.'

'Sí.'

'Is that all you're going to say?' She was stunned when he swept past her, the air all but crackling with the anger that was rolling off those broad shoulders of his.

Following him out into the kitchen, she watched him fill the kettle and set it to boil.

'All right. Because you have done me this service I will accept your so-called "ground rules". I will pretend that we did not join together as man and woman and I will keep my association with you strictly impersonal. Is that what you wanted to hear, Sabrina?'

Trailing her hand over the cold marble counter-top, she briefly nodded. 'Yes, it would be easier.'

'Easier for who—you? Because you are afraid of life, of really living. Because you feel safer hiding behind a social mask even in your private life. Yes…I can see how that would be easier for you.'

His stark words lashed at her soul like a whip and she actually felt herself flinch. How could he know so much about her when he had only known her for the shortest time?

'I'm not afraid of life; of living. I'm only thinking of the best thing to do for everyone concerned.'

His rage was tangible. 'Do not presume to speak

for me as if you know what is best for me. You clearly do not!'

'I'm sorry to make you so angry. How can we resolve anything if we can't even talk to each other without getting in an argument?'

'You think this is an argument?' His laugh was short and harsh. 'Clearly our cultures are very different.'

Her voice trembled. 'I'm beginning to see that.'

Dropping his shoulders, he seemed to take pity on her. 'Don't worry, Sabrina, I will not make any more "inconvenient" demands on you. We will conduct this marriage like a business merger and that is all. Does that make you happier?'

'Yes.' *Liar!* her heart protested. 'Thank you.'

'As far as I can see, you have nothing to thank me for. *Nada!*' His black eyes blazing, he swept out of the kitchen without giving her so much as a backward glance.

'Well,' Sucking in a deeply shaky breath, Sabrina fought hard to keep her composure. 'That went well…'

Making coffee in the end room, Sabrina heard Javier get up, open the door and tell Jill that he was going out to get some lunch. When the door clanged shut behind him she closed the lid on the milk carton, opened the fridge and popped it inside without releasing her breath. When she did, it whooshed out of her as if she'd been holding it under water and had only just surfaced in time. Since their little 'talk' personal relations between them had been strained to say the least, but here in the office Sabrina could find no fault in Javier's conduct. He was the consummate young professional, guiding Jill, Robbie and herself almost effortlessly round the new programme he had installed with ease, making the difficult seem simple, answering their questions with a display of understanding that belied his mere thirty years on the planet. They quickly learned that he was a natural leader as well as a natural innovator and they were all enthused by his suggestions for making the company more competitive in the marketplace while retaining the long-honed skills they had acquired themselves on the way.

But still Sabrina felt unaccountably hurt by the fact that he'd gone to lunch alone. When he rang half an hour later to inform Jill that he'd bumped into a friend and would be away longer than he'd thought, Sabrina's mind jumped into overdrive.

Who was this 'friend'? Was it someone Michael had known or was it perhaps one of the parents from Angelina's school? Until he returned an hour and a half later she couldn't concentrate on a damn thing and when he did return and looked at her with a cool, almost dismissive glance across the top of the computer monitor, her insides turned to ice. Determined to devote her complete attention to the young woman planning a backpacking holiday in India who was seated in front of her with her boyfriend, she conjured up her best, most professional smile and pretended it didn't matter that Javier D'Alessandro clearly no longer regarded her as a friend.

On her way home later that evening, Javier having left before her, Sabrina found herself heading towards one of the big chain shops that specialised in modern, trendy clothing for youngsters. Estimating Angelina's size, she picked out a couple of nice sweatshirts with the shop logo on and a pair of jeans and hoped the child would like them. Her purchases packed, she then headed towards a favourite bookstore that housed a welcoming coffee-shop and, after browsing for a good hour, finally settled at a chrome table to drink a café latte and flick through the books she'd bought. While she'd been active it had not been so difficult to push thoughts of Javier from her mind, but, once seated, her shopping bags at her feet and her books piled beside her on the table, she felt strangely hollow at the thought that he was giving her the cold shoulder—at home at least.

Sipping her latte, she wondered if she hadn't made things even more difficult for herself by insisting they keep their relationship strictly professional. And why was he so angry with her anyway? The man could surely have any woman he desired in a heartbeat. Why he should want a work-oriented thirty-seven-year-old who hadn't had a decent relationship in longer than she cared to remember, she couldn't begin to fathom. Was it just because she happened to be sharing the same living space as him? After all, wasn't it a given that some men found it easy to have sex without getting their emotions involved? The sooner the adoption went through the better, as far as Sabrina was concerned. Her heart ached at the thought of leaving the child, whom she'd really grown to care for, but ultimately she knew it was best in the long run. One day Javier would meet someone more suited to his age and status, and in all likelihood add to his little family. Once she'd paid him back the money he'd given her for the business—and she did intend to pay it back, every penny—then Sabrina would be nothing but a dim, distant memory.

Glancing down at the time on her slender gold watch, she knew she couldn't put off going home any longer and braced herself for another difficult evening with the man she had so recently married.

CHAPTER EIGHT

CRADLING his glass of wine between his hands, Javier gazed thoughtfully at the beautiful woman sitting opposite him, her long legs drawn up on the sofa beneath her, her softly tousled black hair drifting across her elegant shoulders in her tight strapless dress, and wished she were miles away in Buenos Aires instead of here.

'I cannot advise you about whether or not you should marry Carlo, Christina. Only you can judge that. If you are asking me whether I think the marriage will last then that is another thing entirely. He is already paying alimony to two previous wives who have six of his children between them, no?'

The sultry woman pouted and picked off an imaginary piece of lint from her leopard-print dress. 'People can change, Javier. You must know that. Look what you have had to do. You have had to leave your luxurious apartment in Buenos Aires and all your friends and come and take up residence in this cold, rainy country and be a father to Angelina as well! Plus you have had to marry some plain, frigid Englishwoman so that you can stay here! I do not know how you can bear it all, *querido*—I really don't!'

'Plain' and 'frigid' were not words that a man could ever use to describe Sabrina, Javier thought, his blood quickening—even if she had withdrawn every bit of her previous warmth towards him in order to maintain the supposedly required distance between them. As Christina was talking he kept glancing at the clock on the mantel, wondering where she had gone after work and what was keeping her. Angelina had been looking forward to her coming home this evening but now the child was tucked up in bed, fast asleep, clearly unconvinced by her uncle's explanation that Sabrina would be home soon, he was sure. She had probably just decided to work late, he'd told his niece. Now he was all knotted up inside, wondering where she was or—more importantly—who she was with. OK, so he wasn't looking to make this marriage of theirs a permanent fixture and God knew he was not in love or anything like that—but he did have certain feelings for this woman who had answered his prayer in his hour of need. And it was his duty as her husband, real or not, to make sure that she was safe.

'Querido?'

Snapping out of his reverie, Javier took a sip of his now slightly warm white wine then with a grimace put it aside on the small occasional table beside him. 'I'm sorry, Christina. I have a lot on my mind at the moment. Forgive me.'

'I was so sorry to hear about poor Michael. I only met him a few times but I always thought he was a nice man. It must have been a blow, *sí*?'

It took an almighty effort to force away the heavy black cloak that he sensed settling around his shoulders. Michael's death had been a terrible blow—Christina had guessed right—and Javier missed the fact that he could no longer talk things over with his brother-in-law the way he used to. Instead, whenever his thoughts turned to Michael or Dorothea, there was such an ache inside him that it almost left him breathless. That was why he had vowed never to get too close to anyone he cared about again. Angelina, of course, being the exception.

'I am living in his house.' He shrugged, dark eyes absorbing the family photographs on the mantelpiece, the baby grand piano by the window that Michael had loved to play whenever he got the chance, the bookcases stacked with biographies and medical books—Michael's favourite reading. 'All around me are reminders of him and Dorothea. They were happy here. Now they are both gone. It is hard to be here, I will not deny it, but I have to be strong for Angelina. When the adoption papers come through I will be her father and we will both have a new life.'

'And this woman…your temporary "wife"—she will go?' Christina held her breath. She knew she wanted to be with her darling Carlo but she wouldn't be a woman if she didn't still have a certain attraction to the beautiful man who had wined and dined her in some of the most exciting capital cities in the world. And, looking at him now, his brow creased and his eyes full of sorrow, she had no doubt he was in need of some comfort. The kind of comfort only a woman could supply. Uncurling her long, slim legs from beneath her, Christina padded across the luxurious carpet in her stockinged feet and settled herself next to Javier on the arm of his chair.

'Sí,' he said, glancing up at her glossy crimson mouth, 'she will go.'

'Querido.' Sliding her long, elegant fingers beneath his jaw, Christina bent her head and kissed his cheek.

When she attempted to bestow a second kiss—this time on his lips—she felt him stiffen and pull away. Shock radiated through her like a slap.

'I have missed you, Javier,' she told him, her voice deliberately low. 'Have you not missed me too? Just a little bit?'

He remembered walking into his apartment, hearing laughter from the bedroom, pulling the door wide and seeing Christina naked against the pillows while the ageing, paunchy figure of his neighbour, Carlo Andretti, lay beside her, smoking a cigarette. The memory made him sick to his stomach. He pushed to his feet to pace the room, glancing again at the clock, feeling impatient and angry because Sabrina hadn't come home yet.

'You are welcome to stay the night, Christina. There is a guest room already made up. But tomorrow you must go back to your hotel. Apart from taking Angelina to school, I have many things to attend to so I will not be able to keep you company.' Not least of all, telling Sabrina and her staff that they would have to close the shop for at least three or four weeks while the extensive refurbishment was carried out. He knew Sabrina was hoping to avoid such a decision but plainly she could not carry on working with workmen replacing windows and ripping up floorboards all around her. The refurbishment was part of the modernisation programme to give the agency a whole new, much more professional look—a look that would hopefully bring in a lot more customers to boost business. If he hadn't stepped in when he had, Javier had no doubt East-West Travel would be trading on goodwill alone and soon even that would dwindle to nothing.

'All right. I understand. You are still mad at me for finding me with Carlo, *no*? But you were always working, Javier. Working or travelling. A woman gets lonely for a man when that happens.' Moving across the room, her small, slim body in the tight fake leopard-skin dress an eye-catching contrast against the pale, muted colours of the room, she bent deliberately slowly to pick up her high-heeled strappy sandals, then, smiling seductively, moved up close to Javier. 'Show me the way to your guest room, then. I am too tired to wait for a taxi to take me back to the hotel.'

Relieved that she was retiring for the night at least, even if she wasn't taking his preferred option of returning to her hotel, Javier gladly took her down the thickly carpeted corridor and up a short flight of stairs to the guest room.

Careful not to wake anybody, Sabrina tiptoed down the darkened corridor to the kitchen and, flipping on the light, laid her parcels carefully on the table. Stripping off her damp raincoat and pulling the tortoiseshell clip from her hair, she also kicked off her shoes then crossed the tiled floor to put the kettle on to boil. After her shopping trip was over she hadn't felt brave enough to return home to Javier and Angelina so instead she'd driven to her flat, opened some windows to let in fresh air, watered her plants and collected a few more belongings to bring back with her. When she'd done all that, she'd sat back in her armchair to rest for five minutes before starting for home and had promptly fallen asleep. When she'd woken an hour later, the wind was blowing an almighty draught through the opened windows and the room was freezing. Rousing herself, she'd closed them tight, given the flat one final check to make sure everything was in order, gathered her belongings and got back into her car.

Concentrating on pouring hot water from the kettle onto some coffee grounds in a cheerful pink mug, she almost scalded herself at the sound of Javier's deep, rich voice at the door.

'I will get a towel for your hair. You are wet.' Disappearing momentarily, he returned to the kitchen just as Sabrina was taking a careful sip of her steaming coffee, her pulse accelerating at the sight of him dressed in dark jeans and a black polo-neck.

He handed her the large sky-blue towel and she put down her drink. 'Thanks.' Shivering slightly, either from her damp hair or the sheer tension of sharing the same air space as her husband, Sabrina briskly rubbed her hair, knowing she should really head for a hot shower and dry it properly, but too tired to even contemplate it.

'You went shopping?' He jerked his head towards the various carrier bags and parcels on the table, relieved to know where she'd been but still anxious to know why she had returned home so late.

'It's not something I indulge in very often,' she replied a little defensively, hoping he didn't think she'd been spending some of the money he'd given her for the business. 'Now and again a little retail therapy doesn't hurt.'

His dark gaze lingering on the unconsciously sensual way the silk of her blouse stretched taut over her breasts as she stretched upwards to dry her hair, Javier manfully absorbed the hot sexual jolt that shot through his body and told himself not to forget that Sabrina's new ground rules were now apparently in operation.

'Implying that there is an emotional need not being met, *sí*?'

There was something terribly erotic about the way he pronounced the innocent Spanish word. Folding the towel over the back of a chair, she ran her fingers self-consciously through the tumbled weight of her honey-brown hair, her eyes curiously bright. 'Still playing amateur psychologist, Javier?'

His laugh was low and husky. 'Is that what you think I'm trying to do, Sabrina, figure you out?'

Turning back to the mug of coffee she'd left on the counter-top, she glanced vaguely back across her shoulder. 'Do you want a drink? The kettle's just boiled.'

He hated the knowledge that she was suddenly uneasy with him and wished he knew how to put things right, to make her realise he wasn't going to pounce on her as soon as she let her guard down. A yawn catching him unawares, he stretched his arms high and shook his head. 'No, thank you. I think I will go to bed now that you are home. We have a busy day ahead tomorrow.'

'Thank you for waiting up, but you didn't have to.' Her hands tightened round the pretty pink mug and she wished her spine didn't feel quite so tight every time she looked at him.

'It is my pleasure.' With an enigmatic look at her startled gaze, he smiled. 'Goodnight, Sabrina. Sleep well.'

* * *

Angelina tipped out the smart bag with the new clothes Sabrina had bought her, rifled through them, then excitedly held up a bright red sweatshirt to her chest. 'Thank you, Sabrina. They are lovely. I'll try the jeans on tonight when I come home from school.' With a shy grin, she moved round the table to give Sabrina a slight peck on the cheek.

Flushing with pleasure, Sabrina was almost unbearably moved by the little girl's spontaneous delight. Her gift was such a small thing and she hadn't expected such a warm reaction. Tucking her unbound hair behind her ear, she parted her lips in a relieved smile. Drinking her tea in her dressing gown, she reached out to squeeze Angelina's hand. 'I guessed your size but if they don't fit I can take them back and change them. Maybe you'd like to come with me and choose something yourself?'

'All right, then, but I'm sure they will fit. They look fine.'

'And I'm sorry I wasn't home last night in time to say goodnight.' Sabrina's brow creased guiltily as she silently wished she hadn't let her uneasiness with Javier prevent her from seeing the child.

'That's OK. As long as you came home and you were all right.' With a shy glance back she returned the clothes to the white bag with the famous black logo on it and, at a shout from Rosie to come and brush her teeth, left Sabrina in the kitchen to contemplate the day ahead alone. It touched her more than she could say that Angelina expressed pleasure in her coming home. When the time finally came for her to leave the little girl and her disturbing uncle, Sabrina knew it was going to be one of the hardest things she'd ever done, but surely Javier wouldn't mind if she kept in touch—to see Angelina at least?

She was contemplating all of this and more when Javier entered the room. Already washed, shaved and dressed in an immaculate black suit, the tang of his aftershave wafting seductively round the kitchen, he was the epitome of a rich, successful young entrepreneur, and Sabrina self-consciously pulled the neckline of her terry robe closer together, feeling a peculiar vulnerability around him that she wished would go away.

'Good morning. Can I get you something to drink—tea? Coffee?' Starting to rise from the table, she was waved back down again with an engaging smile that made her suck in a deep breath to steady herself.

'I am fine, thank you. As soon as you are ready we will get going. There is a lot to do today and I am anxious to make a start.'

Javier liked the sight of her clothed in the long white terry robe, her beautiful golden-brown hair rippling softly down her back and her face scrubbed clean of make-up. Right now she was a million miles away from her image as a smart, efficient businesswoman, which he sensed she was most comfortable with. By the wide, slightly unsure expression in her beautiful blue eyes, he knew she could not have been more ill-at-ease in being discovered in such a way.

'I'll go and get myself sorted out, then.' Just as Sabrina got to her feet, a woman she'd never seen before in her life swept into the kitchen behind Javier, spun round and demanded he help her do up the zipper on her very inappropriate strapless dress. As Sabrina stared, open-mouthed, Javier obliged without a word—his movements calm and unhurried as if it was the most normal request in the world. Her fingers digging into the table-top, Sabrina's knees started to shake. It was true she had told him he should get on with his own life, even see other women if he wanted to, but, God help her, she hadn't thought he would actually act on it. The woman in the tight dress was raven-haired and beautiful, exquisitely made up with slightly almond-shaped black eyes that gave her an undeniably exotic look. In her comfortable terry robe, her face unwashed and her hair not yet brushed, Sabrina couldn't help feeling like some scruffy bag lady who'd accidentally wandered in on the perfect couple from a glossy magazine. Had Javier slept with this woman last night? Had she been waiting in his bed when he'd bid Sabrina goodnight?

'Sabrina, this is a friend from home. She's working in London for a few days and dropped in to see us. Christina, meet my wife—Sabrina.'

The black-eyed beauty's luscious red lips parted in a purely fake smile. 'So you are the helpful Englishwoman who came to my darling Javier's aid? I am very pleased to meet you…Sabrina.'

Sabrina's head started to throb and suddenly she wanted to get out of the bright, warm kitchen, where previously she'd been relaxed, and escape to her room. 'If you'll excuse me, I have to get ready for work.'

She was out the door before Javier could waylay her and, hearing him call her name, Sabrina just headed straight for her room, barely taking a breath.

Her lungs hurt by the time she pulled open the door and slammed it behind her, and she fell back against the wooden panelling with her heart pounding and an acute pain slashing through her ribs. *Jealousy.* She was jealous, angry and betrayed. How could he sleep with another woman under the same roof as her when the one thing she'd been so sure of was that he was one of the most honourable men she'd ever met?

'Sabrina! Let me in…please!'

He was banging on the door, rattling the brass door handle. Swallowing down the pain in her throat, she took a deep gulp of air before replying, 'Go away, Javier. Just let me get ready for work. Please!'

'It is not how it looks, Sabrina. Christina is an old friend. Nothing happened between us last night, nothing. She came to visit and it got late. She was too tired to go back to the hotel so I let her stay here.'

'Old friend, huh? How old? Twenty-four, twenty-five?' She couldn't believe how pathetic she sounded. *Get a grip, Sabrina, for goodness' sake!*

'Are you going to let me in?'

'No! I'll see you at the office. Don't wait for me; I'll make my own way there.'

'Dios!' With a final thump on the door, she heard him stride back down the hall.

She'd frozen him out all morning and as soon as Jill and Robbie had gone to lunch and the shop was empty of customers, Javier followed Sabrina into the little back room, leaning against the doorjamb as he watched her make coffee and arrange some sandwiches on a plate.

'You will have to stop being mad at me very soon.

It is not fair on Jill and Robbie to have to work in such an atmosphere.'

Pouring milk into her drink, Sabrina stirred it vigorously with the little silver-plated spoon. 'I am not mad at you,' she said evenly. 'It's entirely up to you who you sleep with. I just expected you to have a little more class than to do it while I was sleeping under the same roof.'

Javier bit back some curse words in Spanish that sprang to his lips. 'And I thought you had more class than to take out your anger on the people who work for you. I thought you took pride in your professionalism?'

That cut her to the quick, even more so because it was true. That didn't, however, prevent Sabrina from venting her spleen on the man who dominated the doorway. His handsome face deceptively calm, she could none the less see the spit of fire in those devastatingly dark eyes and she resented it. Resented it mightily when she was the one who had so clearly been wronged.

'How dare you?' Before she knew she even intended it, she'd walked right up to him and poked her finger in his chest. 'How dare you talk to me about professionalism when you come home and act like some two-penny Lothario? *I* was the one who was trying to behave with some kind of dignity by striving to keep our relationship purely on a business level only! Then because I tell you I'm not going to make a habit of sleeping with you, you have to go and pay me back by bringing another woman into the house!'

'Madre del Dios!' Fury slamming into his gut, Javier stared down into her accusing blue eyes as

emotion finally got the better of him. He'd done everything in his power as far as he could see to make her see sense, to explain about Christina, why she was in the house, that she was only in London for a few days, that she was flying back to Argentina to be with her lover, Carlo. But none of it had apparently convinced his wife that he would never stoop to such a low act as to sleep with another woman just because Sabrina had withdrawn her favours. And why was she getting so angry anyway when it had been her own suggestion that they keep their relationship strictly professional? *Unless she was jealous.* The thought sideswiped him, made his heart beat a little faster and sent heat heading right where he didn't want it to go.

'Do you want me, Sabrina?' His voice dropped to a much lower, huskier cadence. He saw the shock in her eyes, the perfect blue dilate to almost black. He caught her hand mid-air, on its way to slap his face, no doubt. 'Is that what all this is about?'

'Of all the arrogant, conceited, chauvinistic—' He cut off her stream of words with a hard, savage kiss that had her falling against him to keep her balance. With his hands in her hair he held her fast, his mouth devouring hers, showing no mercy, only satisfied when with a desperate little groan she melted into him, her arms slipping almost helplessly round his neck, her skin hot and her breasts pressed tight into his chest.

He wanted her so badly he couldn't get enough of her. She had him burning up with lust, this woman who presented such a cool façade when inside she was pure fire. *Dios!* Did she really believe he could have another woman in his bed after tasting her?

Dragging his mouth away, he set her aside, with frustration tensing every finely honed muscle in his body, his face set into determined, angry lines.

'I am going out for some fresh air. When I return I expect you to treat me with the civility that—as your husband—I am due. No more of this ''freezing me out''. Is that understood?'

Her mouth still throbbing with the passion of his kisses, in fast danger of losing her centre of gravity, Sabrina stared at him wide-eyed, her silky hair drifting loose from its clip. 'You have no right to speak to me like—'

'I do not wish to stand here arguing with you. If you want an argument, save it for when we get home and Angelina is asleep. *Sí?*'

His gaze sweeping over her face with barely controlled fury, Javier turned and walked away, leaving Sabrina feeling curiously as if she'd just survived a cyclone.

CHAPTER NINE

'WHAT am I supposed to do for three weeks? Sit around and twiddle my thumbs?' She was spoiling for a fight and Javier knew it. Sitting in front of the TV, one long leg draped across the arm of the chair, he flicked it off with the remote and sighed. They'd already had this 'discussion' once tonight and clearly Sabrina hadn't come to terms with the idea that her precious agency would be closing for such a long time while the refurbishment got underway. Jill and Robbie, on the other hand, had been delighted.

'Why don't you think about a vacation? When was the last time you took any proper time off, Sabrina?'

Folding her arms across her chest, she walked in front of him, a tense, slender figure in jeans and white shirt, her pretty hair left loose down her back. 'That's neither here nor there.'

'Don't give me one of your enigmatic answers. Tell me the truth.'

'Why? So you'll come to the conclusion I'm such a control freak I'm afraid to take any time off from the business in case something goes wrong in my absence?' It was true. She hadn't taken a holiday in over three years, for exactly the reason she had so eloquently outlined. Ironic when she ran a travel business.

Raising a dark eyebrow, Javier couldn't resist a smile. 'How long, Sabrina?'

'Three years. The last break I had was in Tunisia three years ago. Satisfied?'

Come and sit on my lap and let me unbutton your shirt and I might start to be… Coming out of nowhere, the thought had him instantly hardening. He pulled off his tie, dropped it on the chair arm and adjusted his position. 'You should think about it. That is all I am saying. The work will not take place for another two weeks or so, so you have plenty of time to think about what to do with your time off. If you are so eager for contact with work, I could show you how my business works on the internet. Perhaps you would like to learn, hmm?'

Sabrina felt a ridiculous rush of pleasure, quickly followed by a surge of guilt at being so testy with him, then a wave of anger at the thought that maybe he was just trying to placate her after the Christina debacle.

'It's always useful to learn something new.' Her voice sounded grudging even to her own ears. What was it about this man that had her emotions seesawing around so crazily? She'd always thought of herself as quite a reasonable person, a *forgiving* person. With Javier she was being anything but. Outrageous when he had already given her so much.

Javier sighed and got up from the chair. 'Talking of work, I have a few things to see to. If you will excuse me I will say goodnight to you, Sabrina. Sleep well.' He had to put some distance between them in order to think. It wasn't going to happen while she was so near. *Sweet temptation with a scowling face.* It didn't look as if she was going to forgive him any time soon for what she believed to be his serious transgression with Christina. Well, he would just have to wait it out. She couldn't stay immune to him for ever, could she? Frowning as he reached the door, he didn't risk a glance over his shoulder at the object of his desire. He'd already had enough provocation for one day.

But Sabrina had no intention of letting the matter lie. Convinced he had slept with his glamorous ex-girlfriend when she'd stayed the night, she had to let him know that, fake marriage or not, she wasn't going to be made a fool of so easily. Returning to her bedroom, she collected the box of pretty lingerie Javier had bought her and swept into his office with it, slamming it on the desk in front of him so that the gorgeous oyster-coloured silk spilled out onto his lap. His broad shoulders visibly tensing, Javier picked up the flimsy items and put them carefully down on top of the silver box without speaking.

Unable to contain her anger any longer, Sabrina glared at him. 'And don't buy me things like this when it's clearly just a game to you! I tell you what, why don't you give them to your girlfriend? I'm sure she could find a use for them when you next get together!'

Slowly, Javier got up from his chair. Sabrina saw the warning flinch of muscle throb in his cheek beneath the smooth, tanned skin and her heart missed a beat.

'They are not Christina's size,' he said, his voice deadly even. 'She is all angles, while you are more...' those deep black eyes of his swept almost insolently down her figure '...more curvaceous. Why are you so angry with me, Sabrina? You are the one who was so certain that this marriage of ours should be—how do you say?—platonic. So why does it bother you that I might have slept with Christina? A man has needs, Sabrina. Is that what scares you so? I can see how that might prove a challenge when you have locked away your feelings for so long. Do you intend to spend the rest of your life pretending not to feel?' When he reached out to stroke his knuckles down her cheek, Sabrina hugged her arms around her waist to stop herself from shaking. She had known him such a short time yet he already knew her so well. Perhaps *that* was what scared her the most?

'We—we had a deal, an agreement.' The words suddenly didn't mean a damn thing any more. Floundering in her anxiety, Sabrina sensed all the fight drain out of her. This man had already been through so much. He had lost his sister and his brother-in-law and was now totally responsible for his niece—so much so that he had given up his glamorous lifestyle in Argentina to move to England and adopt her. What he didn't need was any further grief from Sabrina just because her pride had been hurt. He was a very virile, sexy man. Having been a recent recipient of his lovemaking, she could easily attest to the truth of that. No. She would just have to accept the fact that, as he said, 'he had certain needs' and if she wasn't willing to fulfil them herself, then who could blame him for finding solace elsewhere? Even if it was with his ex-girlfriend?

'I'm sorry.' Her head throbbing, she swung round to leave, surprised and shocked when Javier's hand fastened round her arm to waylay her.

'I did not make love with Christina the other night.

I have no reason to lie to you about that. She is in love with another man back home in Argentina. I found them in bed together and that is when our relationship ended. I have no desire or intention to renew it.'

Her cheeks burning, Sabrina nodded slowly. He was telling her the truth. She knew that now.

'I've made a fool of myself, haven't I?' Her blue eyes looked pained.

'No. It is good things are out in the open. Go and get some rest now. I will see you in the morning.'

When he released her arm and turned away, Sabrina was crushingly disappointed. She wanted… no, *needed* him to kiss her. Her whole body ached for it—to feel that incredibly soft yet sometimes hard-looking mouth sliding across hers, sharing his heat, his passion, his incredible taste with her, as intimate as a man could be with a woman.

'Can I—can I take my things?' Biting her lip, she reached around him to pick up the pretty silk from his desk, the material cool and unbelievably erotic beneath her fingers. Without a word, Javier handed her the box, the ghost of a smile flitting across his lips, gone as quickly as it had appeared. 'Thanks.' Not daring to encroach any further on his good will, Sabrina hurriedly exited the room, her own heartbeat pounding heavily in her ears as she rushed down the softly carpeted hall to her bedroom.

'So what will you do with yourself with three weeks off?' Taking a generous bite of her authentic Italian pizza with its extra topping of Parmesan, Ellie glanced speculatively at her sister across the table.

The popular Italian restaurant was full of lunchtime customers and Ellie had had to book a table so they could eat there. She'd left the children at her mother's and was enjoying her 'me time' enormously, as she told Sabrina.

'Javier's going to teach me a bit about his own business.' Pouring some water from the jug into her glass, she took a brief sip, wishing that her body wouldn't get so inconveniently hot at just the mention of her husband's name. Usually all her concerns were to do with work, how things were going, how to improve things, where she was going to get the money to make some much needed changes. Now that all that was taken care of, all she seemed to be able to think about was Javier D'Alessandro. For someone who had never given a personal relationship with a man top priority in her life, that was unsettling indeed. It was going to make it all the harder to leave when the time came—not to mention leaving Angelina…

'God, you've got a one-track mind, sis!'

'What do you mean?' Terrified that Ellie might have discovered her guilty secret—that she was more than halfway in love with her husband, a fact that she was only just allowing herself to admit—Sabrina stared at her, wide-eyed.

'All you ever seem to think about is work! There you are with that gorgeous hunk of man and the only thing you can get excited about is the prospect of working together! I'll never understand you in a million years, Sabrina, I really won't. And why aren't you eating? Your pizza will get cold.'

She couldn't eat, Sabrina thought miserably. Not when her stomach was so tangled up with thoughts of Javier and Angelina and how empty her life was going to be without them.

'I keep telling you that our marriage isn't real. We only did it to help each other out. When are you going to get that through that thick skull of yours?'

'Don't give me that "our marriage isn't real" bunkum. I know desire when I see it and you two could barely keep your eyes off each other the day I visited. I told Phil. Talk about a match to a fire! Come on, Sabrina, be honest—you fancy him, don't you? If you don't then I really recommend a medical check-up because your equipment can't be functioning properly.'

'Can we change the subject?' Pushing at the pizza on her plate with her fork, Sabrina was blushing profusely. What she felt for Javier wasn't just some sordid little 'it will blow over' sexual itch. Her feelings for the man went so much deeper than that it wasn't funny. Right now it was threatening the very fabric of who she'd imagined she was for the past thirty-seven years. Her chosen course in life had been her career—*not* marriage and children. Now Javier D'Alessandro had her seriously contemplating both and she had no right. He was still young and he deserved to find someone more in keeping with his age and background.

'You care about him, don't you?' Taking a sip of water, Ellie placed her glass carefully back down on the cork mat. 'Is that what's going on? Talk to me, Sabrina. I don't just want to pry into your business. We're family. I care about you.'

'Why wouldn't I care about him and Angelina? I'm not made of stone.' Shaking her head, Sabrina crumpled her paper napkin into a ball. 'I didn't mean for it to happen. It's not the cleverest thing I've ever done.'

'But human, very human. Why wouldn't you want love in your life? Isn't that what we all ultimately want—someone who really cares about us deeply?'

'But he doesn't love me.' Hastening to make that very clear to her sister, Sabrina felt choked just saying the words. 'He might be attracted to me but that doesn't mean it's anything more than physical. And besides, I'm too old for him.'

Ellie looked militant. 'Who says?'

'*I* say! Think about it, Ellie. In a few years' time he'll want children. He comes from a very old-fashioned culture where family is sacrosanct. Do you think his parents would be happy if he married a woman who couldn't bear him children?'

'All this is supposition. You don't even know for a fact that you can't have children. You could pop out at least three or four if you got your skates on!'

Laughing in spite of her anguish, Sabrina reached across the table to cover Ellie's hand with her own. 'You are a nut. But at least you make me laugh. I get so wrapped up in the business sometimes I seem to forget how to have fun.'

'Have that conversation with the gorgeous Javier. I'm sure *he* could teach you how to have fun.'

'Hmm.' Thinking about the beautiful lingerie he had bought her that she had retrieved after her little contretemps the other night, Sabrina didn't doubt that was true. What had he been thinking when he bought it for her? Her insides glowed at the thought. 'Dangerous.'

'Hold that thought.' Attracting the attention of a passing waitress, Ellie ordered a bottle of house red. 'You need to learn to loosen up a little, my girl, and this is going to help.'

'No,' Sabrina wagged her finger, '*this* is going to make me fall asleep at my desk.'

'Why worry? Your husband's there to make sure you get home OK, isn't he?'

Returning to the living-room with two mugs of black coffee, Javier stopped in the doorway at the sight that met his eyes. Curled up on one end of the huge couch, her head on two satin pillows, Sabrina was fast asleep. At the other end, curled up in a similar fashion, was Angelina—also asleep. His insides suffusing with warmth, he took a long, slow breath and, advancing into the room, placed the coffee on a sideboard. Standing there watching them both, he couldn't disown the sudden longing in his chest to hold these two females in the circle of his love and protection for ever. The thought almost made him stumble. It was natural he should feel such tenderness towards Angelina; he'd loved her since she was a baby and soon she would be his adopted daughter. But to acknowledge such feelings towards Sabrina—this woman who had appeared out of nowhere, as it were, just when he needed her? This was something else entirely, something he definitely hadn't planned for. She was a beautiful, vibrant, sensual woman and he desired her with a depth that had surpassed anything he'd ever experienced before, but love? He'd sworn to protect his heart from such a fate. Angelina and his parents had his unconditional love but to fall for a woman and bind her to him with promises to love her for ever was something he'd vowed not to do, not unless he was looking to get his heart badly broken. He only had to remember Dorothea and Michael to know that love could also be cruel. At thirty years old he had had enough tragedy in his life. No. He made up his mind. He was not averse to enjoying a warm physical relationship with the beguiling Sabrina but, as far as anything else was concerned, he would resist. Gazing at her now, her long, luxurious hair spilling onto the vivid cerise of the satin pillow, he knew it was going to take every ounce of will-power to keep his vow.

She awoke to the gentle sounds of a Joni Mitchell record, the room bathed in the intimate glow of lamp-light, and as she struggled to sit up she rubbed her hand around her neck to ease the tight cramp in her muscle. Disorientated, Sabrina glanced round the room, seeing the royal-blue velvet drapes drawn against the night, the fire hissing brightly in the grate with its comforting crackle and Javier nursing a glass of some amber-coloured liquid between his hands as he stared into the flames from his armchair.

'What time is it?'

'Ten to midnight.' For a long moment he stared into his glass, then slowly he raised his head to regard Sabrina's half-reclining form.

'So late?' Rubbing the sleep from her eyes, she wished her head didn't feel so groggy. 'You mean I've been asleep here since we came back from work?'

'Too much wine at lunch, you said.' A flicker of a smile crossed his handsome face and Sabrina groaned at the admission. Swinging her legs carefully onto the floor, she tried in vain to tidy her dishevelled hair, instead found her clip buried somewhere halfway down her head, rescued it and silently vowed to be a lot tougher in future when it came to her sister's unwise recommendations.

'I try to make it a rule never to drink at lunchtimes. It's fatal. It always makes me fall asleep when I do.'

'You seemed happy when you came back to the office.' The memory gave Javier a decidedly warm feeling. He had seen a very different Sabrina after a glass or two of wine. She'd spent the rest of the afternoon smiling and giggling at him and the customers alike and finally Javier and Robbie had had to take charge while Jill had led Sabrina safely into the little back room and made her drink a large mug of black coffee.

'Yes, well, I promise I won't make a habit of it. Drinking at lunchtime, I mean.' Getting to her feet, she briefly lifted her hair off the back of her neck then stepped forward towards the fire. 'This is nice.' Crouching down beside the crackling flames about a foot away from where Javier sat, she held out her hands then rubbed them up and down her arms to get her circulation going again because she'd felt chilled when she'd woken.

Her hair was haloed by the light from the fire and Javier studied her exquisite profile and felt heat of a very different kind suffuse his body. Taking a sip of his brandy, enjoying the burn that rippled satisfyingly along his throat to his stomach, he offered the glass to Sabrina. 'Have some.'

'What is it?'

'Brandy. Very good French brandy.'

'I'd better not.'

She watched mesmerised as Javier slowly dipped his finger into the glass, wetted it and offered it to her instead.

For one crackling, electric moment, Sabrina didn't know what to do. Her stomach muscles clenched so tight that she almost forgot to breathe. Her eyes huge, she leant forward a fraction and circled her hand round his wrist. She was aware of his white shirt cuff and the onyx cufflinks outlined with gold, the fine black hairs on the back of his bronze hand, the faint spicy drift of his aftershave as she lowered her mouth to capture his finger between her lips.

She heard the low rasp of his breath as she slowly licked her tongue along his flesh then released him, tasting brandy and Javier, feeling light-headed and so aroused that her nipples were erect to the point of pain against her blouse. Then her fevered brain registered the softly seductive Spanish as he moved off the chair and got down on his knees beside her. His eyes were very dark and completely intense as he cupped her face between his hands.

'What is it about you that makes you so hard to resist, Sabrina?' Lowering his mouth, he kissed her gently, experimentally, making her heart zing and her eyelids flutter closed. Curling her hands round his wrists, she eased back to look at him, knowing she could easily ask him the same question, but maybe it was a question she already knew the answer to? He had the kind of 'sit up and take notice' good looks that made women glance knowingly at each other when he walked into a room and smile at the fantasy of sharing his bed. His bearing was relaxed, confident, bordering on arrogant. But it wasn't an empty, shallow kind of confidence—Javier D'Alessandro more than delivered the goods. Not only was he clever and hardworking, but he also had integrity and honour that would put lesser men to shame, as well as being kind to children and women who needed a prayer or two answered. Everything considered, he was a pretty irresistible package all round.

'We said we weren't going to do this,' she whispered softly. One of the logs on the fire cracked and spat and Sabrina held her breath as Javier stroked down her cheek with the pad of his thumb. His eyelashes were very black—almost with a blue sheen—and she could see the tiny lines that fanned out from the corners of his eyes.

'Rules were meant to be broken, *no*?'

She was about to agree when a child's distressed cry cut through the room, making them both spring apart and jump to their feet.

'Angelina!' Javier was out of the room before Sabrina got her bearings. She found him kneeling beside Angelina's bed—the child's hand in his while his free hand stroked her brow. Even at the door, Sabrina could see the little girl was pink and flushed, her dark eyes shimmering.

'She is burning up.' His voice sounding almost unbearably hoarse, Javier threw her an anguished glance and Sabrina hurried towards the bed to feel the evidence for herself.

'Hello, sweetheart,' she soothed, brushing the

child's hair back from her face, 'aren't you feeling well, darling?'

'My head hurts.'

When Angelina gazed at her as if she was about to burst into tears, Sabrina put her hand on Javier's shoulder. 'Get a bowl of tepid water and a flannel.'

He was already halfway to the door when he stopped. 'Tepid?'

Seeing the confusion in his eyes, Sabrina elaborated quickly. 'Not too cold. If it's too cold it might give her a shock.'

'Sí.' He was gone and back again in no time. Taking the flannel and wringing it out gently in the water, Sabrina sponged Angelina's feverish brow as Javier looked helplessly on.

'I've checked her over for any rash,' she said quietly, remembering the instructions for signs of meningitis pinned to Ellie's huge American-style refrigerator. 'And there doesn't seem to be anything untoward. Right now we just need to bring her temperature down. Can you look in the medicine cabinet for any Calpol or paracetamol? And wake Rosie; she might be able to help too.'

'It's Rosie's night off. She's gone to visit a friend at university in Brighton. She won't be back until tomorrow.' Driving his hand impatiently through his hair, Javier stared worriedly down at his niece. She'd thrown off her bedcovers and the pretty pink duvet was bunched round her knees. In the soft glow of the night-light Sabrina pulled it up a little over her nightdress and continued to sponge her heated brow. 'She's very hot. If this doesn't work soon we should call the doctor. You have the number?'

'Of course I have the number. I will ring now.'

He disappeared before Sabrina could say any more.

'You're going to be just fine, my angel. Just fine, I promise.'

'You won't leave me?'

Seeing the anguish in her face, Sabrina squeezed her hand tight. 'Are you kidding? I'm going to stay right here all night if I have to. You don't get rid of me that easily! Once I care about someone I stick like glue, I can tell you.'

Angelina's brief, tentative smile tore at her heart. Silently offering up a prayer, Sabrina smiled back, reminding herself to breathe, to stay calm, not to show even the slightest anxiety to the little girl she had grown so fond of.

'He said about half an hour.' Anxiety creasing his smooth, tanned brow, Javier crouched down beside Angelina then dropped an infinitely tender little kiss on her flushed cheek. 'You are going to get well, *mi querida*. I promise. The doctor will not be long.'

Angelina's eyes fluttered closed. Sabrina glanced at the man beside her, her chest feeling tight when she sensed the worry rolling off him in waves. He had already lost so much—his sister, then Michael. No wonder he looked so gripped with fear. Her hand came down on his shoulder and stayed there awhile. 'It's probably just a bug she picked up at school. It happens all the time. She's strong, Javier—she'll get better in no time. I'll stay with her tomorrow. Jill and Robbie can manage for a day without me.'

'Then we stay here together,' he said, not looking round at her but staring at the sleeping child on the bed instead. 'Nothing matters more than Angelina being well again.'

CHAPTER TEN

AFTER two days of worrying himself into a stupor over Angelina, Javier knew he had to start resuming an iron resolve as far as his feelings for Sabrina went. The woman had stayed home from work on both days to help take care of his beloved niece because Rosie had also come down with a bug and advisedly stayed put at her friend's. In the end she'd ministered to both of them, reassuring Javier with words of comfort and hot soup when he refused to eat anything more, and nursing Angelina the way a devoted mother would her child. It was the latter that had him convinced that she was a dangerous woman to be around. Already, he had more than lost his heart to her and it terrified him to finally realise the state of his feelings.

As for Angelina, after two days of being too poorly to leave her bed—a viral infection, the doctor had proclaimed—today she was tucked up on the big couch in the living-room. By her side on the floor there was a virtual Aladdin's cave of videos and DVDs to choose from, and her uncle had left her laughing at a cartoon with Sabrina, who'd popped home for lunch to see how she was, while he mooched around the kitchen trying to come to terms with his emotions. If his adoring mother so much as suspected her son's growing attachment to the woman who'd married him in name only, she'd be on a flight out of Buenos Aires so fast to make sure he held on to her that his father would be left eating her dust.

His brow furrowing at the thought, he glanced up at Sabrina's soft-footed entrance. In one of her plain but smart business suits, her hair coiled up behind her off her collar, some tiny pearl studs in her lobes, she looked the kind of woman a man could depend on—and not just in a business sense. After the past two days, Javier knew Sabrina was capable of so much more. She was cool and calm in a crisis, and more to the point didn't buckle under pressure—even when it was something she was hardly used to handling. If there was ever a woman who was made to have children, it was she. He was convinced of that much.

'She's looking much better today, isn't she? More like her old self.'

'My heart is glad.' The simple statement carried a wealth of meaning. The child meant everything in the world to him. It gave Sabrina a bitter-sweet pang to know how much, because it made her wonder what it would feel like to have someone care that passionately about her.

'You look better today too. I see you've had a shave.' The corners of her pretty mouth kicked up and so did Javier's pulse.

Grinning wryly, he rubbed his hand around his clean jaw. 'I did not want to frighten you away by looking like Blackbeard, *no*?'

'Funny, but I could see you as a pirate.' It wasn't funny at all, Sabrina realised with a little jolt of heat in her stomach. It was downright licentious! Javier as some marauding pirate looking dark, dangerous and disreputable—it was a fantasy that should be purely reserved for night-time. It had no business interfering with her thought processes during daylight hours. Not when she had to get her skates on and go back to work.

'Anyway, I have to go. I've got a customer coming in to talk to me about visiting Iceland of all places. Just saying the name makes me shiver. As if it wasn't cold enough!'

She was babbling to hide her discomfort. Did he even guess how hard it was for her to behave normally in his presence? After two days in the closest proximity, sharing the worry and concern of a sick child, both letting down barriers they'd rarely let down before, it was becoming more and more difficult to contemplate leaving—and that was *without* taking the lovely Angelina into consideration.

'We will have a take-out tonight, I think. You look tired and I do not want you worrying about cooking. Rosie will be back tomorrow. I had a phone-call this morning so hopefully things can return to normal. Take care of yourself, *sí*?'

Unconsciously his voice had lowered and, venturing a smile, Sabrina took a step back towards the door. 'You too.'

Poring over the take-out menu for a local Thai restaurant later that evening, Sabrina glanced up in surprise at the sound of the doorbell echoing through the house. Leaving Angelina's bedroom, where he'd just gone to check that she was sleeping peacefully, Javier called out, 'I'll get that.'

As her gaze returned to the menu, Sabrina's hand fluttered to her complaining stomach. She was starving. For the first time in two days she actually felt like eating. Now it seemed her appetite had caught up with her with a vengeance.

'Sabrina. You have a visitor.'

Blinking in disbelief, she straightened to see the bustling, concerned figure of her mother enter the room, with Javier close behind her. Joan Kendricks was smaller and plumper than both her daughters but her eyes were as blue as theirs while her hair, although faded to grey, was prettily highlighted with becoming streaks of ash blonde. She smelled of Chanel No. 5, as she usually did, and Sabrina noted she was wearing one of her best dresses beneath her smart black wool coat.

For a moment, her daughter just stared in shock.

'Mum! What are you doing here?'

She was in the process of laying some shopping bags down on the big pine table, and Joan Kendricks' neatly plucked eyebrows flew up towards her hairline. 'It's nice to see you too, Sabrina. What did you expect? That I'd leave you to your own devices when I heard the child was sick? What kind of mother do you take me for?'

The child? Ellie must have said something, of course. Sabrina had spoken to her sister a couple of times while she was at home nursing Angelina.

'And good of you to introduce me to your new husband as well.'

Her heart in her throat, Sabrina stared wide-eyed at Javier across her mother's shoulder. He shrugged and grinned but did not look half as discomfited as Sabrina felt.

'I'm sorry, Mum. This is Javier—Javier D'Alessandro.'

'You're a brave man, taking this one on.' Joan swung round to survey the tall, handsome man who reminded her of one of those old-fashioned matinée idols of the fifties, and firmly shook his hand. 'She's too independent by half.'

'Tell me about it.'

He was smiling…*smiling*, would you believe? Joan smiled back then proceeded to shrug off her overcoat. Wordlessly, Javier took it and disappeared briefly to go and hang it on the coat tree in the hall.

'Anyway, how is the poor little thing? Angelina, I think Ellie said.'

'She is doing very well,' Javier answered. 'She is sleeping now and well on the way to full recovery.'

'I'm glad to hear it. Would you mind if I took a little peek? Just to satisfy myself.'

'No. Not at all.'

'Sabrina?'

'Yes, Mum?'

'Put away that take-away menu. What the pair of you need is some proper food. I know what it's like to nurse a sick child and it's easy to neglect your own needs. In one of those bags you'll find one of my big dishes with a casserole in it. Pop it in the oven and give it a good twenty minutes' heat-through. In another bag you'll find a bottle of champagne. It should be well chilled because I've had it in the fridge at home all day but pop it in yours anyway, there's a good girl. I'll be right back as soon as I've had a look at the child.'

As Sabrina automatically began to sort through the

bags on the table, she stood-stock still all of a sudden, dazedly shaking her head as if to convince herself that she hadn't imagined the scenario that had just taken place. 'Thanks a lot, Ellie!' she breathed out loud. No doubt Javier was already trying to come to terms with that 'just run over by a steamroller' feeling, a state of mind both Kendricks girls were well used to when it came to their mother.

Ten minutes later, the casserole simmering nicely in the oven and fragrant smells permeating the kitchen to mouth-watering effect, Sabrina sat at the table, sipping her coffee, her stomach in knots, wondering what on earth her mother and Javier were finding to talk about.

'What a beautiful child!'

They returned to the kitchen, Joan pulling out a chair to sit opposite her daughter, while Javier switched on the kettle and sorted cups and saucers from the dresser.

'Now, come and sit down, young man. We'll have tea or whatever it is you're making later. Sabrina, open that bottle of champagne and fetch three glasses.'

About to rise from the table, Sabrina dropped back down into her seat, scowling. 'What's all this about, Mum? What's the champagne for? You rarely even take a glass of wine.'

'Listen, it's not every day my elder daughter gets herself married, is it? Even if I wasn't invited to the ceremony I would still like to celebrate with a glass of champagne. Ellie was right when she said your husband was a lovely young man. As soon as she told me I knew everything would be all right. You'll do very well together, I can see that.'

Her heart sinking, Sabrina dared a glance at Javier. He was leaning against the dresser, his arms folded across that gorgeous chest, apparently as relaxed and at ease as if it were his own mother who had dropped by for a visit. But it wasn't safe to make assumptions about anything, was it? He might be hating every second, squirming inside because her mother had clearly got hold of the wrong end of the stick. Hadn't she explained to her that she'd married Javier simply to help him get a British passport and stay in the country? So what on earth had made her suddenly assume it was some kind of match made in heaven?

'Mum, please!'

'Oh, you think I'm embarrassing your young man?' Joan chuckled as she tilted her head towards Javier. 'He's not embarrassed in the slightest, are you, dear? Besides, he'll have to get used to my ways. He's part of the family now.'

Javier produced the glasses, three elegant flutes, while Sabrina got the champagne out of the fridge and plonked it on the table. Even though the whole thing was farcical, she would have to go along with it for now because she quite honestly didn't feel up to facing a scene after the last few days. All of a sudden she was feeling desperately tired, like a favourite old cardigan that was suddenly looking too worn out to wear again.

'Well.' Her blue eyes crinkling at the corners and looking as though she might cry any minute, Joan Kendricks raised her glass to Javier and Sabrina. 'Here's wishing you both a long and happy married life. I must confess I was always afraid that my beautiful Sabrina would end up alone; all she seemed to think about was that business of hers.' She glanced at Javier confidingly, her glass still poised in the air. 'That's not to say that her father and I aren't proud of what she's achieved, but I did fear it wouldn't be enough, if you see what I mean. Nothing can replace children and a good man. So anyway, lots of love to you both.'

'Gracias.' His expression unreadable right then, Javier toasted his mother-in-law and his wife in turn, his dark gaze boring into Sabrina as she felt herself blush what must have been a deep beetroot-red. In her top ten of most embarrassing moments, this surely had to be number one? Here they were, drinking a toast with her mother to a marriage that Sabrina and Javier knew was destined to have a very short shelf life. Both pretending that it was something true and honest worth celebrating, while inside Sabrina feared her heart might break if she had to pretend any longer. The truth was she was desperately in love with Javier and couldn't imagine her life without him. Which was tough when that was the outlook that beckoned—like it or not.

'Now, you two,' rising to her feet, Joan patted her hair, 'I'm going to love you and leave you and let you enjoy your dinner in peace. When Angelina is properly well, I'll come and visit again and bring your father if I may, Sabrina? Having met your charming husband, I'm sure George would also like to have the pleasure of his acquaintance. I'll give you a ring, sweetheart. That OK?'

A bit difficult to say 'no, everything isn't OK now

that you've been and caused emotional mayhem,' Sabrina thought wearily.

'You will be more than welcome.' Flashing her mother one of his delectable 'stop a woman in her tracks' smiles, Javier helped her on with her coat, then walked to the door with both women. Watching Sabrina obediently proffer her cheek for her mother's parting kiss, he was surprised but not taken aback when Joan pulled his shoulders down and kissed him soundly on his own cheek.

'Take care, now. See you soon.'

'Well, that was disastrous!'

Following his wife back into the warm kitchen, Javier creased his brow in bewilderment. 'I do not understand.'

'You see what I have to put up with? The woman wants to run my life! She thinks she can just waltz in here and—'

'Sabrina. Your mother brought us a meal. She brought us champagne and asked to see Angelina. What can be disastrous about that? As far as I could see, all she was doing was behaving like a mother. I saw nothing wrong in that.'

'And what about that ludicrous toast of hers, hmm? What did you think about that? She knows full well this is only a temporary arrangement yet she deliberately buries her head in the sand and pretends she doesn't! I wouldn't blame you if you were furious.'

'Well, I am not.' Picking up his glass of champagne, he took a sip. 'Your mother understands the importance of family, *sí*? You cannot blame her if she only wants the best for you. My mother would be the same.'

'What *she* thinks is the best for me, you mean. You heard how she alluded to my business? Almost as if it was some kind of failing on my part instead of an achievement. Her only goal is to see me as a contestant for ''mother of the year''. She won't be satisfied with anything else, don't you see? Just because I wanted to make my own way in life and not depend on some man to keep me, I must be lacking as a woman in some way. Ellie already gave up her career in preference for being a wife and mother; don't you think she'd be satisfied with one daughter doing what she wants?'

'Are you so against the idea of being a mother? A wife?'

His question, so reasonably asked, cut through the red mist in Sabrina's brain. Her gaze trapped by his slow, steady perusal, her tongue came out to moisten her lips.

'No. I'm not against it. I just don't think it's for me.'

'Too set in your ways, you said.'

What would he say if she simply confessed she was just too damn scared? Scared of not coming up to scratch, scared of failing, of not being enough. At least with her business she knew where she stood.

'You can still be a success in your chosen career and be a wife and mother. In my opinion something would suffer, but that's only because I think the children's welfare should be paramount—at least while they are small the mother should stay at home if she can and take care of them. A child needs stability.'

Something poor Angelina had lost. Now it was up to Javier to provide the stability and love that had been ripped away so cruelly. There was no doubt in Sabrina's mind he was more than up to the task.

'Why is it that whichever way I turn I feel as if I'm in the wrong?' Stupidly she felt like crying. If only her mother hadn't chosen this particular evening to drop by and toast their marriage, because the experience had left Sabrina wishing with all her heart and soul that her marriage to Javier could be real.

'You are not wrong because you have a different opinion. I know how much the business means to you, Sabrina. That is why I want to help you. At the end of the day you have to do what is best for you.'

'And what *is* best for me, Javier? Do you know what's best for me? Because I sure as hell don't!' She'd flown from the room before he had a chance to stop her and Javier put down his drink, dug his hands deep into his trouser pockets and wished his mother or sister could be here so that he could ask them to explain about women…

As he stood in front of Michael's walk-in wardrobe, Javier's gaze settled on all the tightly packed Savile Row suits and knew he could no longer ignore the fact that they were there and something had to be done. He had no intention of wiping out every sign that Michael had ever lived in the house, but he was certain that as long as there were too many visible reminders both he and Angelina would find it hard to make a new life. So he had to make a start. The first thing he would do would be to pack up all the contents of Michael's wardrobes and drawers, and anything that wasn't obviously personal or that Angela Calder didn't want he would donate to a local charity shop. That done, he would get some quotes from decorators and think about redecorating both Michael's and Angelina's rooms. He would, of course, involve his niece in the design process and hopefully get her excited about planning a new look for her bedroom. He had had a little chat with Angelina before she went to sleep last night and they had both decided it was too soon to start searching for a new home. They would stay in the house until the summer at least, and maybe then they could think about moving.

Javier deliberately didn't allow himself to dwell on Sabrina's position in all of their plans or even if she would be involved. All he knew was that she had cried herself to sleep last night after refusing him entry and he had lain awake in his room down the corridor with his door opened, listening to her muffled weeping, his chest so tight that his breathing felt impeded. When she'd left for work this morning, her usual peaches-and-cream complexion looked pale and drawn and there were soft smudges of grey beneath her dulled blue eyes. Whatever was going on in that fertile mind of hers she hadn't wanted to share it with her husband, and Javier had watched her leave the house with a heavy heart, knowing that sooner or later it was all probably going to end in tears.

Refusing to think about that now, he started to remove the suits from the wardrobe, glad to have something to keep both his hands and his brain occupied or else he would definitely go crazy.

'How are you feeling today, sweetheart?' Joining the child and her nanny in the living-room on her return from work, Sabrina bent low to the couch to kiss Angelina on her smooth, plump cheek. The little girl seemed happy and healthy, tucked up beneath her red tartan blanket watching television, Rosie sitting beside her companionably, munching a packet of crisps.

'Much better, thanks. Tomorrow I'm going to get up properly because my friend Julie is coming over.'

'Good news, eh? And how are you, Rosie? I was sorry to hear you weren't well.'

'I know.' Rosie's eyes rolled heavenwards. 'Bad luck that I was laid up the same time as poor Angelina. Still, it was lucky you were here to help her uncle look after her, wasn't it?'

'It was.' Clutching her bag to her chest, Sabrina forced a smile. 'Where is Javier, by the way?'

'In Daddy's room,' Angelina replied, her gaze fixed on the TV screen in the corner of the room. 'He's been clearing out things so that we can decorate.'

'Oh.'

Having changed into jeans and an old chambray shirt, Sabrina knocked on the door of what was once Michael Calder's bedroom and, hearing the terse 'Come!', cautiously stepped into the room. There seemed to be piles of clothing everywhere, on the chair, on the huge canopied bed, on the highly polished Victorian chest of drawers. From the opened door of a walk-in wardrobe, Javier appeared, his black hair mussed, his blue shirt opened at the collar with his sleeves rolled up, his long legs encased in soft, dark denim jeans with a black leather belt cinching his waist. He was scowling and didn't exactly look pleased to see her but the scowl only served to highlight his inevitable attraction. Inside her chest, Sabrina's heart gave a crazy little leap.

'Need any help?' she asked.

'No. I have everything under control.'

'You are angry with me?'

'No.'

'Then would you like something to eat? I bought some steaks and the makings of a salad. Even *I* can't mess that up.'

He didn't smile at her joke and her stomach lurched. 'What's wrong?'

Even though he briefly turned his face aside, Sabrina didn't miss the flash of pain that passed across his eyes. Michael. How could she have been so insensitive as to walk into the room that had once been his brother-in-law's, see the clothes that had once belonged to the man piled up ready for removal, and not realise that her husband was hurting, missing the man who had once been his friend—the man who had been married to his beloved sister…?

'Nothing is wrong. Leave me. I will come and join you shortly.'

'Javier, I—'

'Go, Sabrina! Can you not understand that I do not want you in here?' His black eyes were blazing, and she felt his fury hit her somewhere in the solar plexus. Swallowing down her hurt, she decided to stay her ground. This wasn't about her. This was about the man who had sacrificed his own dreams, his way of life, to come and take care of an orphaned little girl because she was family.

'What if I don't want to go, Javier? What then?'

He swore in Spanish, shook his head, then started to pull open one of the drawers in the Victorian chest. Her heart pounding, Sabrina walked up behind him, slid her arms around his waist, felt his whole body stiffen in protest, then leant her head gently against his back. Her senses were immediately invaded by the warmth and the scent of the man, making her realise just how much she had been longing to touch him like this.

'What are you doing?'

'What does it feel like I'm doing?' she murmured.

'Dios!' Pushing her arms away, he spun round, his expression furious. 'I told you I did not want you in here.'

She blinked. 'I don't believe you. You need me.'

'I do not need anybody!'

'You're lying.'

'Sabrina, I—'

Drawing level, she curled her hand into his shoulder and drew his face down to hers. Before he could react, she slanted her mouth deliberately across his, coaxing his tongue, drawing his silky heat into her own, then slid her free hand down his shirt, passed the leather belt round his waist, and boldly down to the now bulging fly of his denim jeans.

Moving his mouth from hers, he slid it in a damp trail across her cheek to her ear and Sabrina registered his helpless shudder with a small flare of excitement deep in her belly. Murmuring a destroyingly sexual entreaty against the tender skin of her lobe, he lifted his head to stare deeply into her wide blue eyes. 'Go and lock the door,' he commanded hoarsely.

CHAPTER ELEVEN

WHEN she came back he swept her down onto the soft blue carpet, his hands already on the buttons of her shirt, pulling it aside—feasting his gaze on the soft, creamy mounds of her breasts in her white lace bra.

'So,' he said softly, 'you will not share with me what is in your mind but we will share this, hmm?'

Even as he spoke, he was undoing her zipper, tugging at the heavy denim as he tried to rid her of her jeans. In a fever of desperate wanting, Sabrina helped him, then, urging his mouth down to hers, lost herself in the hot, deep flavours of his kiss, the hard, warm male textures of his skin. Feeling the taut muscles of his shoulders bunching beneath her palms, she realised he was reaching for his own zipper, easing it down, with one firm tug divesting her of the matching white lace panties she was wearing.

Reaching into his back pocket, he sheathed himself with the contents of the small foil packet he withdrew, then, positioning himself more fully on top of her, staked his claim with one sure, deep thrust, emitting a gravel-voiced groan as his hips ground against the firm but soft flesh of her thighs. Sabrina shut her eyes, murmuring words that were more like prayers—words she'd never uttered to any man before Javier. He consumed her; not just with his amazing body, but with his mind and his heart and his soul as well.

He was a good man, the *best* man, and she loved him with a depth of feeling and emotion that had been beyond her experience until now. It was terrifying how much she loved him. But oh, how she craved for him to love her back, craved as much of him as he was willing to give and more. As he thrust deeper, the ache for him growing into an unstoppable crescendo, her fingernails dug into the coiled steel muscle of his biceps as he brought her to climax, her body digging deeper into the soft blue carpet beneath her with the force of his possession. With a harsh, heavy groan, his own release quickly followed, his body pumping harder into hers as she sagged, spent, against the floor, her mind spinning, her body throbbing in the aftermath of the torrid, urgent coupling that had just taken place.

As he dropped his head onto her chest his warm, ragged breath whispered tantalisingly across her breasts in the white lace confines of her bra, and even though she was still dazed from his loving she wanted his hands on her again, skin to skin, breath to breath. Consumed by love, Sabrina pushed her fingers through the short, silky strands of his black hair. 'Are you all right?' she asked him gently.

He lifted his head, his dark eyes glittering back at her with hunger and sorrow and something else that she couldn't quite reach.

'You ask me if I am all right?' His perfectly even white teeth looked even whiter against the smooth bronze of his skin. 'It is I who should be asking you that question. I confess I had planned on a long, slow, sweet seduction some time soon before I completely lost my mind with wanting you—but this?'

Apparently furious with himself, he made a move to detach himself, but Sabrina stroked across the rippling muscle in his arm beneath his shirt and her lips parted in a softly coaxing smile.

'Passion has a life of its own, you said. Remember?'

Nodding slowly, he gazed down at her lovely face, those bewitching blue eyes with their sweeping honey-brown lashes, the soft pink flush on her cheeks. '*Sí.* I remember.'

'Then don't be angry.'

'I am not angry with you.' In one fluid movement he detached himself from her, grabbed a handful of tissues from the box on the chest of drawers, disposed of the condom then pulled up the jeans that he hadn't removed completely. Then, reaching for Sabrina's scattered clothing, he dropped the items gently down across her belly. 'It is the world in general I am angry at—maybe God too. I cannot help wondering what else the powers that be have in store for me.'

'Only good things, Javier. I am sure of it.'

'I am not sure of anything right now. I miss the wisdom of my friend. Michael always seemed to know the right thing to do in a crisis. After Dorothea died, people were amazed at how well he coped; how he was able to soothe others even in the depths of his own grief—me included. But I knew his heart was broken. That is why he never married again. In eight years I think he had one or two dinner dates—that's all. He was not interested in any other woman except my sister.'

Sucking in a shaky breath, Sabrina clutched her clothes to her stomach then slowly started to put them on. 'He must have loved her very much.' Her voice husky, she couldn't bring herself to look at him. The sorrow in his voice made her want to protect him from every hurt that ever came his way again. It made her want to throw herself into his arms and tell him how desperately, how deeply she loved him, that she could understand Michael not wanting anyone else after Dorothea because she felt the same way about Javier. But she couldn't tell him that, could she? Not when they'd made an agreement. And Javier wasn't ready to surrender his heart—she could see that—not when he associated loving someone with losing them.

'I'll make us a nice meal.' Touching his shoulder as she walked up behind him, she sensed his relief that she was bringing this conversation to an end. 'Will you join me in a while?'

'Sí.' For a moment the heat of his gaze scorched her and she couldn't look away, then he lifted his hand, smoothed back a lock of her hair and sighed. 'Thank you, Sabrina.'

But as she left the room, Sabrina wasn't exactly sure what it was he was thanking her for.

'William, darling, don't cover Auntie Sabrina in flour, please! She's got to go back to work very soon.'

With two huge, meltingly blue eyes staring wonderingly up at her beneath a shining curtain of precision-cut blond hair, Sabrina grinned at the little boy who up until a moment ago had been liberally dusting flour from his mother's baking all over the kitchen floor, and wished with a sudden fierce longing that he was hers. The yearning for a child of her own had been slowly creeping up on her ever since she'd met

Javier and the delightful Angelina and there didn't seem to be anything she could do to put a stop to it. Consequently when she'd woken early that morning with stomach cramps that were bad enough to press-gang her out of bed and into the bathroom, she had hugged her arms tightly around herself and cried shamelessly at the visible proof that she couldn't be pregnant. It didn't make sense. The ordered, tidy, safe little world she'd so carefully constructed around herself for the past fifteen years had been totally turned on its head and she didn't feel as though she had a hope of righting it any time soon.

'He's all right. He's just being creative, aren't you, William? He might be a top chef one day, you never know.'

'Just as long as he makes loads of money and keeps his mother in the style to which she could easily become accustomed, eh, Will?' Reaching for the broom, Ellie began to energetically sweep the trail of flour dust into a corner before scooping it up in a dustpan. From the living-room Tallulah's sudden indignant wail cut through the house and Ellie pushed back her hair and rolled her eyes at Sabrina.

'Kids, eh? Who'd have 'em? I expect Henry has lobbed something at her, as usual. I can't seem to make him realise she's not some kind of bendy toy doll that won't break.'

Following her sister into the topsy-turvy living-room that was turned upside-down by an earthquake of clothes, books, toys and half-nibbled discarded biscuits, Sabrina watched Ellie stoop to pick up the distressed baby from the playpen while little Henry plonked himself on the carpet and picked up a rattle, apparently oblivious to his sister's cries.

'There, there, now. You're all right. Mummy's here, darling girl.' With a kiss on the top of her head and a firm cuddle, Ellie's practised ministrations quickly soothed the baby's crying, and as the child pressed her face into her mother's faded green T-shirt Sabrina once again had to hold back the tide of emotion that threatened to overwhelm her.

'You're looking a little peaky if you don't mind me saying.' Her brow puckering, Ellie suddenly narrowed her gaze suspiciously at Sabrina.

'Oh, my God! You're not—?'

'No, I'm not.' Kneeling down beside Henry, Sabrina coaxed the toddler into her arms, sitting him down on her lap with the baby's rattle. 'For goodness' sake, you're as bad as Mum. When are the pair of you going to get it through your thick skulls that this marriage of mine is only temporary? A business arrangement?'

'Who are you trying to kid? It's as plain as the nose on your face, Sabrina Kendricks, you're loopy about the man! And if I'm not mistaken—and I *know* I'm not—he feels exactly the same about you. And if you're telling me that you've spent all this time under his roof and haven't done the deed then either your libido has ground to a halt from lack of use or you're an even slower worker than I thought you were when it comes to men!'

'Thanks.'

'Don't mention it. And by the way, that hurt look doesn't wash with me either. You're in love with him, aren't you?' Her voice softening, Ellie joined her sister on the carpet, carefully sitting Tallulah down in front of her to face Henry.

'What do you want, a signed confession?' Sabrina's blue eyes looked pained.

'Have you told him?'

'Are you mad? Of course I haven't told him!' At Henry's startled glance, Sabrina hugged the child to her, ruffling the top of his baby-fine hair with her fingers. 'Javier doesn't want to get involved with me that way. He's lost his sister and his brother-in-law and Angelina is his priority, and nobody could blame him for that. The last thing he needs is an emotional entanglement with a woman eight years older than him and a workaholic to boot.'

'You're not a workaholic. You *used* to be, but since you've met Javier you've changed, Sabrina. Can't you see it? We were lucky if we got to see you once a month, let alone once a week. Now you drop by fairly regularly and when you do you mainly talk about Javier and Angelina—a sure sign that work is no longer your big priority.'

Ellie was right, Sabrina realised. Of course, East-West Travel was still important, but somehow, without her knowing, her priorities had changed. Javier and Angelina had become her family without a doubt and they *did* take priority in her life. So much so that it was going to be an unbearable wrench to leave them behind—as one day soon she would have to. And somehow she knew that, no matter how successful her business became, nothing would ever compensate for the awful loss of the man and child who had come to mean so much to her.

'Well, it won't do me any good. He's not ready to get involved with me. He's hurting too much.'

'Of course he is. He's not going to get over something like this in five minutes, that's obvious, but with you by his side you can teach him how to trust again, Sabrina—how to love someone without fearing for their life, because that's what's at the root of this, isn't it? It has to be, otherwise he would have told you he wants you to stay.'

Expelling a softly shaky sigh, Sabrina swallowed down the lump in her throat. 'How can you be so sure? Javier could have any woman. He's rich, successful…God knows he's good-looking—why would he want me?'

'Honestly, Sabrina, listen to yourself! Is your opinion of yourself really that low? You are a gorgeous, successful woman in her prime—why *wouldn't* he want you?'

'You've never thought of me as successful—you or Mum.'

'What utter rubbish!' Ellie's arms crossed her chest in exasperation. Both Tallulah and Henry looked wonderingly at their mother. 'Mum tells all her friends how proud she is of you. She's forever leaving your business cards about the place wherever she goes, for God's sake! At the doctor's, the dentist, on the bus, talking to a perfect stranger…and Dad's the same. And how could you think *I* wasn't proud of you? Whenever I glance in the mirror lately I pray I'll look as good as you when I'm your age, and on the days when my clothes are covered in baby drool or I haven't even had a minute to pull a comb through my hair, don't you think I think about you and feel just a teeny bit envious? There you are with your own business, taking care of yourself, meeting new people every day and looking gorgeous while you do it and there's me resembling something that the cat dragged in! I don't regret motherhood for a second, you know I don't—but I wouldn't be human if I couldn't see the benefits of the path you've chosen, Sabrina.'

'Thanks, Ellie.' She felt as if a huge weight had been lifted off her shoulders by the time her sister had finished speaking. 'We should have talked like this before. I've been such an idiot.'

'Being an idiot isn't exclusively your prerogative, sis. We're *all* guilty of that from time to time. Now go home and talk to Javier—or is he at work with you today? Wherever he is, go and tell him how you feel. I think I can safely promise he's not going to pack your bags and throw you out on the street!'

She'd picked up a film she'd wanted to see for the longest time on her way home, and in her brown leather tote bag there was a very good bottle of crisp white Chardonnay along with a box of sweets for Angelina. Not knowing whether Javier had made any plans or not for the evening, she prayed he wasn't going out, that he would want to share the film and the wine with her and afterwards talk with her a little. Whether she'd be brave enough to do as Ellie had suggested and tell him exactly how she felt, Sabrina didn't know, but she'd promised herself to stop pretending their marriage was in name only, and prayed Javier was ready to do the same.

But all her hopes flew out the window when she arrived home to find Javier's exotic ex-girlfriend,

Christina, in residence in the kitchen. Javier was nowhere to be seen and, apart from the radio playing softly on the counter-top, the house was unusually quiet for that time of the evening. Had Rosie taken Angelina out somewhere? And where was Javier?

Gazing at the sultry woman seated at the kitchen table, flicking through a magazine, her long, very slender legs encased in soft black leather trousers with a silver knit halter-neck on top, Sabrina was suddenly beset by doubt and fear. 'Hello. Where is everybody?' Removing her coat, she automatically folded it across the back of a nearby chair, then moved across the room to fill the kettle for a drink. Anything to keep her hands busy and her brain from going crazy.

'Rosie has taken Angelina to visit a friend and Javier has just popped out to the drug store to get me some headache pills. Are you making coffee?'

Absorbing the slightly condescending glance of the other woman, Sabrina reached up to the dresser for cups and saucers, biting her lip to stop herself from asking the woman why she couldn't have gone out to get her own pills. Who did she think Javier was—her lackey?

'I can do, but is it a good idea if you have a headache?'

'It is not so bad now. I have had a long talk with Javier and am feeling much better. He always knows how to make me feel better. *Always.*'

'He's a good man.' Her back stiff, Sabrina switched off the kettle, spooned some coffee granules into two cups and stirred, all the while her heart thudding with indignation and hurt. Javier had told her that Christina had a boyfriend back in Argentina, that he no longer felt anything for the beautiful model who was his ex-girlfriend. If that was true, why had she shown up at the house again?

'Do you take milk and sugar?'

'No.' Christina's dark eyes flashed as if to say 'do you need to ask?'. 'I have to take care of my figure. It is how I make my living.'

'And is that what you're doing in the UK?' Putting the green cup with its matching saucer down in front of her on a place-mat, Sabrina returned to the counter-top for her own drink. 'Modelling?'

'I did a shoot for Paris *Elle* and decided to make a stopover for a few days in London so that I could catch up with some friends. I particularly wanted to see my darling Javier. When I heard about poor Michael I was glad to come and offer him some comfort.'

Was that what she'd been offering Javier the night she'd stayed at the house? *Comfort?* Sabrina's heart turned over. He'd sworn to her that nothing had happened between them but that clearly wasn't what the sultry Christina was implying.

'He is hot, yes?'

'Hot?' For a moment, Sabrina didn't know what the other woman meant.

'Sexy.' Christina laughed, the sound curiously like a cat purring. 'Good in bed.'

At Sabrina's flustered glance, Christina fixed her with a knowing little smile, her lipstick appearing suddenly too red next to her very white teeth, giving her a hard, almost brittle look.

'Let's not pretend, Sabrina. You have slept with him, yes? I would have been very surprised if you had not. Javier is a very attractive, virile man with Latin blood flowing in his veins. He naturally has needs…needs which only a woman can fulfil. The fact that you so readily agreed to assume the role of pretend wife doesn't stop you from being susceptible to his very apparent charms. But I want you to know that you have not been singled out particularly. Any reasonably attractive woman would have done. I am only telling you this so you do not get your hopes up where he is concerned. When he has been here as long as he needs to be, he will return to Argentina and his family. I know them well, Sabrina, and they would not take kindly to an Englishwoman as their son's wife. Look what happened to poor Dorothea when she married Michael…she was forced to leave everything she knew and loved behind to settle in the UK. Her *mama* was heartbroken. Imagine how she would feel if Javier—her only son—did the same?'

Feeling suddenly chilled, Sabrina leant back against the counter-top and drew her fingers through her softly mussed hair. Pulling out the tortoiseshell comb, she gave it a brief shake loose, willing her chaotic thoughts to start making some sense, trying to get a grip on what Christina was saying, wondering if she ought to take it seriously or if the woman was simply suffering from a case of terminal jealousy where Javier was concerned because she was no longer the woman in his life.

'As far as I understand, Javier's sister wasn't ''forced'' to stay in the UK. It was a choice she made because she was in love with Michael. As for the rest, my hopes or plans are nothing to do with you and therefore not open to speculation or gossip. What's the matter, Christina? Does my being married to Javier pose some kind of threat to you?'

The other woman tossed her head disparagingly. 'Not in the least. I can get any man I wish—Javier D'Alessandro included!'

'Then why did you break up?'

'That is none of your business!'

'Fine. I totally respect your privacy. If you would return the compliment we'll be all square. Now, if you'll excuse me, I've been at work all day and I need to go and take a shower.'

'Well, I'm just letting you know, I may ask Javier to take me out to dinner.'

Pausing at the door, her cup of coffee in her hand, Sabrina threw the other woman a disdainful glance. 'Go ahead. As far as I can see, I don't have the slightest thing to worry about.'

She left the room to a string of Spanish expletives that strangely enough didn't hurt her in the least—even if she had known what they meant.

Relieved to see the back of her, Javier gladly saw Christina into a taxi and waved her a final goodbye. He hoped that he'd made it perfectly clear that she'd outstayed her welcome and there was nothing more between them worth pursuing. When he'd got back to the house with her headache medicine, his heart had almost stalled when he saw Sabrina's bag on the table and her coat over the chair. For all his frantic dash to the chemist and back, he'd been too late to get Christina out of the house before Sabrina's arrival and, judging by the self-satisfied, smug look on Christina's face when he'd asked her if she'd spoken to Sabrina, he knew his ex-girlfriend had probably not missed the opportunity to make mischief. Used to being the centre of attention as far as men were concerned, the beautiful Brazilian model would not like to see another woman have the limelight. Especially when that 'other' woman had ensnared her ex-lover's heart where she had been unable to. Javier had enjoyed their association, as any young man would enjoy escorting a beautiful model around town, but as far as anything else went she left him cold. *Especially* when he'd found her in bed with Carlo Andretti—a man not known for his fastidiousness when it came to personal hygiene.

Drumming his fingers on the table-top, he took a moment to gather his thoughts before going to seek Sabrina out. All day his body had thrummed with the memory of their lovemaking and all day he'd lusted after her in a fever of wanting. She was becoming too important to him for him to simply let her go when his British passport came through and the adoption papers were duly signed, sealed and delivered. What would she think if he told her he wanted to make this paper marriage of theirs real? As real as it could be? Would it frighten her away for good? She was so set on her business being a success, would she find marriage to him and being a stepmother to Angelina too much of a bind or a restriction?

He was willing to recognise that there were no guarantees—the loss of both his sister and her husband had brought that fact tragically home—but he'd put off the moment of truth for long enough and would just have to trust that the outcome would be one that favoured both him and his beloved niece.

That said, he stood outside Sabrina's room for a good two or three minutes before raising his hand to knock on her door.

CHAPTER TWELVE

SHE heard him walk up to her door then...nothing. Pacing the room, her chequebook in her hand, she caught sight of her reflection in the dressing-table mirror as she passed it for the third time, alarmed to see that, yes, she did look as frightened as she felt. Was he coming to tell her that he was taking Christina out to dinner—or, worse, that he and the beautiful Brazilian model were getting back together? Her stomach knotted painfully at the thought. On paper, she and Javier didn't look like the ideal match, granted—but it hadn't prevented her from falling head over heels in love with the man, had it? It didn't prevent her from wondering how she was ever going to take in her next breath if he told her that he wanted nothing more from this marriage of theirs than for her to fulfil her part of the bargain then leave.

Oh, God...what was he doing out there? Why was he taking so long? When the knock on the door finally came, Sabrina still reacted as if a bat had swooped down on her in the dark, and with her heart going crazy she took a deep breath and pulled open the door.

'Hi.'

'Can I come in?' His arms were folded across the impressive span of his chest beneath a dark blue denim shirt matched with his jeans, and his dark eyes roved her face with all the intensity of a man hungry to be reacquainted with his lover. The realisation made Sabrina's world tilt for a disconcerting few seconds.

'Of course. Has your friend gone or have you come to tell me that you're taking her out to dinner?' Presenting him with her back, Sabrina paced across the luxurious carpet to the small padded stool in front of the dressing table, where she turned round again. With anxious blue eyes she waited for his answer.

'Why would I be taking Christina out to dinner?' His hypnotic dark gaze narrowed suspiciously. 'What has she been saying to you?'

'She's very beautiful. I could understand if you wanted—if you wanted to get back together with her.'

'You say this to me when I have already told you she means nothing to me?'

'Then why was she here, Javier? And why were you rushing around getting her headache pills? Is the woman helpless or is it that she's just used to crooking her little finger and the men fall over themselves to do what she wants?'

'*Nada! I* do not come running when she crooks her little finger. She was complaining of a migraine. She said she had left her pills back at the hotel and asked me to go and get her some. I could not sit there knowing the woman was in pain. I would not even do that to a stranger.' Shaking his head, Javier advanced into the room. He looked very big and very angry and Sabrina silently acknowledged that she seemed to have an unhappy knack for igniting his temper. Her legs trembling a little, she dropped down onto the padded stool, folding her hands in her lap and gripping her chequebook.

'I don't want to argue with you, Javier.'

'No?' For a moment there was a glint of humour in his eyes. 'Forget Christina. She is history. Tomorrow morning she will be on a plane home to Argentina. She only came to tell me goodbye. But we need to talk, *sí*?'

'Yes, we do. But first I want to give you this.' She opened the slim grey book, tore out a page and passed it to him.

'What is this?'

'It's my first instalment of our repayment plan. For the money you loaned me for the business,' she explained reasonably.

For a moment he said nothing, just stood staring down at it as if he couldn't comprehend its meaning. Then, lifting his head, staring right at her, he ripped the cheque in two and let the pieces flutter soundlessly onto the floor.

'Why did you do that?' She was genuinely bewildered, her blue eyes widening to saucers.

'I told you I did not want you to repay me. You have already repaid me by agreeing to be my wife so that I could stay and be with Angelina. I do not want your money, Sabrina, so do not insult me by bringing up the subject again. Do you understand?'

'I insist that you take it. I don't want to be under an obligation to anybody. That's not the way I work.'

'No!' His shout almost made her fall off the chair. His handsome face enraged, he stalked towards her. 'Your mother and your sister are right. You are independent to the point of stupidity! While I admire your undoubted ability to stand on your own two feet,

I do not admire this stubbornness of yours to try and prove it at every turn.'

'Well, I don't care whether you admire it or not, it's the way I am, so you'd better wake up and smell the coffee, Javier!'

'Pardon?'

Her bottom lip quivering, Sabrina pushed herself to her feet and swept past him. But she didn't reckon on him reaching out and grabbing her. Nor did she reckon on the hard, hot, punishing kiss that followed. Her heart in her throat, she forgot all about being angry as her breasts were crushed against the warm, impenetrable wall of his chest. Forgot all about obligation and independence and stubbornness and concentrated instead on the feelings and sensations that drowned her limbs like a bath of slow, sweet honey as Javier's mouth took possession of hers and his hands claimed intimate knowledge of her body. Anchoring his fingers in her hair, running them down her back, then cupping her bottom, he moulded her to him with a wild, crazy hunger that tore through them both like a forest fire.

'*Dios!* How did I ever live without you?' Gazing down at her, he proceeded to drop hungry little kisses all over her face, her eyelids, her nose, her cheeks, her mouth, her forehead, until Sabrina's heart felt as if it would surely jump right out of her chest with joy.

'Javier, we still have to talk. We have to—'

'Uncle! What are you doing?'

Startled, they sprang apart at the sight of that little puzzled face in the doorway.

His heart slamming against his chest, Javier considered his niece with a sense of shock, cursing the fates for pre-empting his chance to talk to her about his feelings for Sabrina. Now she would most probably be frightened that Sabrina had replaced her in his affections. How to explain that there was more than enough room in his heart for both of them?

'Angelina, I…'

But the little girl had already turned tail and run, and Sabrina hugged her arms tightly around her middle and wondered if she'd lost the child's trust for good. She prayed not.

'I have to go to her.' His expression undeniably torn, Javier hurried from the room.

Back in the kitchen, Sabrina made coffee that she didn't really feel like drinking then sat aimlessly flicking through the glossy magazine that Christina had left behind. But she didn't really register anything more than a blur of shiny pages because her thoughts were anxious and distracted, and if her stomach churned one more time she'd have to go in search of the bathroom.

'How did I ever live without you?' he'd asked, not knowing that she could have posed the very same question. Now she wondered if she'd left it too late to tell him. If Angelina was too upset by the idea that her uncle had some affection for Sabrina, would he turn his back on his need for her? Would her hopes for the future now all come crashing down around her? And, worse—would she have to walk away from this marriage without telling Javier how much she loved him?

'Sabrina.'

Her heart knocking against her ribcage, she glanced up in surprise at Javier's tall frame towering over her.

'Yes?'

'I've spoken to Angelina.'

'She's very upset? Oh, God, Javier, I would do anything to stop that little girl from being hurt even more. If she hates the idea of me being with you in that—in that way, I'll just give you both more space. I'll only stay until your passport comes through; tell me what you want me to do and I'll do it.' Her hand trembling, she unconsciously smoothed the shiny pages of the magazine back and forth.

Dropping his hands to his hips, Javier registered her agitation, feeling his stomach flare with warmth at the knowledge that Sabrina would sacrifice her own needs for Angelina. He wanted to hold on tight to this remarkable woman and never let go.

'She's not upset, Sabrina, just the opposite. She's delighted with the idea that we have grown to care for each other.'

'She is? We have?' Swallowing down the lump that had lodged in her throat, Sabrina blinked hard, barely allowing herself to dream, to hope.

'*Te amo, Sabrina.* I love you.'

'Javier.' Rising to her feet, Sabrina allowed him to take her hands in his, felt herself engulfed by his warmth and protection, his love, when he urged her head onto his chest. 'Oh, God, I love you too. I don't know what I would have done if you'd said Angelina was unhappy. It would have been so hard—impossible—to pretend I didn't care as much as I did about you.'

'So we are "real", yes? *Mi esposa hermosa.*'

Raising her head to gaze into his eyes, Sabrina

smiled. 'You said that the first time we made love. What does it mean?'

'My beautiful wife.'

'I like the sound of that.'

'You do?' He kissed her forehead, then her nose, then finally her mouth, his lips moving over hers with exquisite tenderness, leaving her in no doubt that he truly loved her. Releasing a shuddering breath, Sabrina pulled away, a frown puckering the smooth, clear skin of her brow. 'You know what people will probably say?'

'Tell me.'

'That I'm too old for you; that I enticed you with my wicked womanly charms; that I married you for your money.'

'Let them talk. They are all lies…except the part where you enticed me with your wicked womanly charms, *sí*?' His hands on her hips, he was urging her against him, heat simmering in those amazing dark eyes of his. 'And you will give me babies…at least two or three, yes? You can still run your precious business—Rosie will be our nanny. What do you think?'

'What if I can't, Javier? Have babies, I mean.'

'Can't is not in my vocabulary. Besides…' he wound his fingers possessively through the soft strands of her pretty honey-brown hair '…we will practise hard. Night and day…whenever we can, *sí*?'

'Sabrina?' Framed in the doorway, her bright pink tracksuit emphasising her tanned skin, her eyes huge and soulful like her gorgeous uncle's, Angelina glanced from her uncle to the woman he held in his arms and back again.

'Yes, Angelina?' Stepping away from Javier, Sabrina dropped down onto the nearest kitchen chair.

Advancing into the room, the little girl planted herself in front of her. Her teeth chewing on her plump lower lip, for a moment she appeared ill-at-ease and uncertain. 'My uncle told me that he is going to adopt me. He's going to be like my daddy. Did he tell you?'

'Yes, sweetheart, he told me.' As she glanced up at the man she loved Sabrina's expression grew even softer.

'Does that mean that when he adopts me you'll be like—like my mummy?'

Oh, God. What was she supposed to say to that? Her gaze naturally gravitated to the tall, brooding man standing behind the child for guidance. She attempted a smile but barely even moved her lips.

'Would you—would you like that, Angelina? I will never take the place of your real mother but I would love you like my own and never let you down, I promise.'

'I think I would like that very much if it means you'll stay with me and Uncle Javier for ever. Will you, Sabrina?'

'Remember what I told you when you were ill? That when I care about someone I stick like glue? Well, when I love someone I stick even harder. You'll never be able to get rid of me now!'

'What do you say about that, *querida*?' Sliding his hand across the child's slender shoulder, he gave it a little squeeze.

'I'm happy. I'm happy that we're going to be a real family. Daddy would have liked that.'

* * *

'I don't care whether you think you know the ending or not, we don't want to know it, do we, Angelina?'

Sitting cross-legged on the floor beside the little girl, her back against the couch between Javier's long legs, Sabrina glanced up at her husband, her blue eyes twinkling with mischief as the television flickered in front of them, the film they were watching well under way. His hands resting lightly on her slender shoulders, he bent towards her head and planted a warm kiss at the side of her neck. A surge of delicious tingling flooded her body.

'No, Uncle, don't tell us the ending. You'll spoil everything!'

'OK, I won't tell you. But only if you let *me* choose the movie tomorrow,' Javier teased his niece. 'This is one of those—how do you call them?—girly films. What I want to see is an action movie.'

'Then I'm afraid you're going to be outvoted,' Sabrina warned him. 'There are two of us girls now so you won't find it so easy to get your own way in future, Señor D'Alessandro!'

'Only in some things, *sí*?' Whispering it for her ears only, he tightened the hands on her shoulders perceptibly. 'When we are alone in our bedroom.'

Sabrina melted.

'Stop whispering all that lovey-dovey stuff to Aunt Sabrina,' Angelina scolded, her face breaking into a delighted grin. 'She's trying to watch the film and you're distracting her.'

'Am I distracting you, beautiful Sabrina?'

Reaching for a handful of popcorn from the bowl on the carpet between herself and Angelina, Sabrina couldn't suppress a happy smile. 'Stop fishing for compliments and watch the film. If your head gets any bigger you won't be able to fit through the door!'

At the sound of Angelina's infectious giggle, Sabrina munched her popcorn and thought with a spurt of satisfaction that family life certainly had a lot to recommend it.

Stepping out of the taxi, Sabrina stood for several moments staring up at the new shop-front while Javier paid the driver, excitement and pride rushing through her with equal intensity. In a few short weeks, East-West Travel had been transformed from a slightly shabby, fading exterior to a smart, up-to-the-minute business that wouldn't look out of place in any modern city centre in the world. Inside, Robbie and Jill were already hard at work and, peering through the window, Sabrina saw that several of the smart easy chairs lined up against the pale cream walls were already taken by waiting customers. It didn't matter that at least one or two had merely come in out of curiosity or to ask for brochures—the point was, East-West Travel had been noticed, and, what with the new equipment and the first-class service both Sabrina and her staff knew how to give, things would soon be thriving. Of that she had no doubt. And none of it would have been possible without the unfailing guidance and support of her wonderful husband.

'Aren't we going to go inside?' Smiling, Javier joined her, automatically enfolding her hand in his. The day was windy and cold but Sabrina was immediately charged with heat at his touch, an occurrence she was happily getting used to.

'I just wanted to take a minute. It's not every day

you have your dream come true, you know.' But she wasn't looking at the shop-front when she said the words. Gazing up into the face of the man she loved, she felt a thrill of dizzying pleasure rush through her body, intoxicating her blood like wine.

'Mi querido,' she said softly.

'My Spanish lessons are paying off, I see,' Javier teased in reply. When Sabrina had told him and Angelina that she stuck like glue to those she loved, Javier believed her. He had lost his heart to this incredible, loving woman but he had no fear where she was concerned. Sabrina had taught him that love was as spontaneous as breathing, there was no limit to the amount you could give so therefore there was no danger that that love would diminish—no matter what happened. Love was infinite and they had the whole of the rest of their lives and beyond to prove it.

'Yes, but I'll definitely need lots more tuition.' Dimpling, Sabrina touched his lips with her fingers and somehow Javier knew his beautiful wife was not just referring to his native language that he was teaching her.

'You are an insatiable woman, Señora D'Alessandro.' His voice husky, he squeezed her fingers and bestowed them with a loving kiss.

Her lovely blue eyes wide, Sabrina laughed in delight. 'You're nearly eight years younger than me, Javier—don't tell me you're running out of stamina already?'

'Never! I will never stop giving you pleasure. *Usted salvo mi vida.*'

As she reached up for a kiss, Sabrina's expression grew suddenly serious. 'You saved my life too, Javier, and I'm going to spend the rest of our lives showing you how grateful I am. That's a promise.'